YOUNG ADULT

MARIAH FREDERICKS

the true meaning of cleavage

Simon Pulse
New York London Toronto Sydney

First Simon Pulse edition June 2004

SIMON PULSE
An imprint of Simon & Schuster
Children's Publishing Division
1230 Avenue of the Americas
New York, NY 10020

Also available in an Atheneum Books for Young Readers hardcover edition.
Designed by Ann Sullivan
The text of this book was set in Garamond 3.

Printed in the United States of America
10 9 8 7 6 5 4 3 2 1

The Library of Congress has cataloged the hardcover edition as follows:
Fredericks, Mariah.
The true meaning of cleavage / Mariah Fredericks.
p. cm.
Summary: When Jess and Sari, best friends since seventh grade, begin their fresh-man year of high school and Sari becomes obsessed with a senior boy, Jess wonders if their friendship will survive.
ISBN 0-689-85092-1 (hc.)
[1. Interpersonal relations—Fiction. 2. Best Friends—Fiction.
3. Friendship—Fiction. 4. High schools—Fiction. 5. Schools—Fiction.
6. Individuality—Fiction.] I. Title.
PZ7.F872295 Tr 2003
[Fic]—dc21   2002006809
ISBN 0-689-86958-4 (pbk.)

For Josh,

who discovered a whole new world for me

> The meeting took place in an ancient grove of oak. They sat among the gnarled roots of a great tree and laid their plans. The future was unknown to them, but they were certain of one thing: Their alliance was strong, their bond unbreakable.
>
> —*Hollow Planet: Destiny's Sword*

I am drawing a picture of Sari Aaronsohn.

Sari is my best friend. But drawing her is harder than you might think.

For one thing, I don't usually draw people. Not real people. I like to do stuff with sci-fi or horror. Intense, with a lot of action. The people I draw usually end up having horns or fangs or webbed feet. I think they're rather cool—but they certainly don't look like anybody you'd see walking down the street.

Not on this planet, anyway.

But I've decided I need to expand my horizons.

Besides, until they let us into the movie, I don't have anything else to do.

I've done Sari's hair, and I'm pretty pleased with it. Sari has easy hair to draw, very dark and tumbly. But her face is more difficult. Partly because right now, it's a pissed-off face. We're waiting on this line to get into *Sudden Death,* which is all about the end of the world and so on. And the line is not moving.

Sari's glaring down the line, like someone's purposely keeping us out.

I say, "Sar, we'll get in. We have tickets."

"I know. But it's taking, like, forever."

She runs the back of her arm over her forehead. It's one of those stinky August days when the sun is like a hammer and the air is like a huge wet hot cloth pressed right in your face. You can't breathe, you feel gross, and all you want to do is get inside, where there's air-conditioning.

See, the thing is, it's our last Saturday of summer vacation, our last day of freedom before we start high school. We have this whole great day planned. I can't blame Sari for not wanting to spend it waiting on line.

Actually, Sari just hates waiting in general.

Looking at my picture, I can't decide how to start her face. I should start with the eyes, because they're definitely what you see first. But then I think I should try something easier, like her chin. A few times, I almost touch the pencil to the paper. But then I chicken out. Glancing at her, I wish she would stand still; it's impossible to really see her when she's turning and twisting so impatiently. I'd ask her to hold still, but I want the picture to be a surprise. A sort of Last Day of Freedom present.

She doesn't notice me drawing. We've been friends

so long, she's totally used to me doodling away.

Finally, I decide to risk it. With one stroke, I draw the entire outline of her face, from the top of her hair to the bottom of the page. Then I look at it, this empty face under a dark storm of hair. I can't figure out whether I've done it right or not.

I suspect I haven't. I suspect I've screwed the whole thing up.

I lean back and close my eyes. The sun is really hot on my face, and I imagine that I'm on a ship, bound for the outer world of Prolus, another exile banished by the Exalted Ones. There is a knife in my boot; the guards didn't find it. The heat isn't the sun, but the engines of the ship . . .

Then I hear Sari shout, "Let us in!" and it's like I'm startled out of sleep.

Sari starts clapping her hands, starts chanting, "Let us in! Let us in! . . ."

The other people on line are giving her looks. You can tell they're thinking, *Obnoxious teenager.* Little glances back and forth: *Oh, let's not sit next to THEM.*

I put my sketch pad away in my backpack and start chanting with Sari. Together we yell, "Let us in! Let us in!" We do a little dance while we chant, swinging our arms and doing kicks on "in," like some kind of crazed Rockettes.

I'm laughing so hard, I can't breathe. I'm wondering how long I can keep this up when all of a sudden, people start coming out of the theater. The line starts to move. As it takes a big leap forward, Sari puts her arms above her head and cheers.

Sari and I have been best friends since seventh grade. We had the same gym class, and we were always the last two picked for every team. Me because I was bad, Sari because she just didn't care. One game, the teacher made Sari be goalie, and she let the ball roll right into the goal. The other team started jumping around and slapping hands. The teacher immediately made her sit down on the bench next to me. I held my hand up, and we slapped hands.

Basically, it was inevitable that we became best friends. We are essentially the only normal people in our entire school, the only girls not obsessed with their weight or hair, the only girls who don't communicate by squealing and squeaking. I mean, there are a few other people not like that. But a lot of people are afraid of the cliques. You can tell they'd like to be accepted by them. Whereas Sari and I despise them and fear no one.

The movie's dumb but kind of fun. I can watch anything that shows you a big black sky with billions of stars, the standard shot of *any* space action movie. In this one, a group of astronauts have to blow up Mars before it hits the earth.

After the movie, I say how there's no way a single bomb would destroy Mars, whether or not you blow it up at the planet's core. Sari says there's no way she would spend her last night alive with Bailey Watts, the guy who played the dudely dude second in command.

As we head toward the bus stop, Sari says, "At your house we're doing the Book, right?"

I nod. "Absolutely."

Sari's sleeping over, and we catch the crosstown bus to my house. While she stares out the window, I go into my knapsack and get out my sketch pad. Looking at my drawing, I see I haven't gotten her at all. Even when Sari's just looking out the window, there are a million things going on in her face. All I have here is some squiggles.

I don't know why drawing real people is so hard, but annoyingly, it is. I think I see it, I think I have it right. Then I try to get it on paper, and somehow, it all just disintegrates. In my head, I know what it should be, but it's like my hands won't cooperate, and nothing ends up the way I saw it.

It's totally frustrating.

Then I notice this guy across the aisle is staring at us. Well, really at Sari. He's not trying to hide it, either.

He's old. Not old old, but way too old to be staring at a couple of kids like us. I stare back, and he looks away.

This happened a lot this summer. All of a sudden, men who could be in college or even married were checking Sari out. Mostly, it was just funny. But one time, a guy ran after us and asked her to marry him. It freaked her out, I could tell.

The bus rolls to a halt at my stop. As we get off, I glance back. The guy's watching again. I give him a look like, *Creep,* and jump off the bus.

I live on the tenth floor of our building. In the elevator, Sari pushes the button for my floor, like she lives there too. Which, frankly, she almost does.

I want to ask her if she noticed the creep on the bus. But I decide not to. It might upset her.

As we ride up, Sari asks, "What do you think the Book's going to say?"

I close my eyes and intone: "The Book must keep its secrets until the time is right."

My parents have gone out to dinner, so the apartment is dark and silent when we open the front door. I call, "Hello?" and hear the *click-click-click* of my dog, Nobo, coming down the hall to greet us. Sari gives him a quick smile. Being a confirmed cat person, she is not entirely wild about dogs.

We order in a pizza and eat it in the kitchen, passing an enormous bottle of Coke between us. Nobo lies under the table, hoping for the best.

"Okay, here's a question." Sari tips her head back to catch a strand of cheese. "Your last night on earth—who do you spend it with?"

I have no answer to this, so I guess. "My family?"

Sari rolls her eyes. "No, I mean, like a guy. Like the movie."

I think. I hate questions like this. Sari loves them.

Sari presses. "Your *last* night on earth."

"James Stewart."

"He's dead," says Sari. She gives me a funny look, like she's worried I don't know this. Or don't care.

I shrug. "Guess I'm out of luck on my last night on earth."

"Come on, what about someone real?" says Sari. "Someone you *know*?"

I made a barfing sound.

"Come on," she says. "Think of everyone you know."

"I *am* thinking of everyone I know."

"You never know," Sari says. "High school could offer some very interesting opportunities."

"Yeah, right, like that's so likely." I take a slug of soda. "What about you? Who do you spend *your* last twenty-four hours with?"

I though she'd have an immediate answer, but Sari thinks about it for a long time.

Finally, she says, "I don't know. I don't think I've met him yet."

Then she sets down her glass. "I think it's time for the Book."

Because it's time for the Book, we don't turn any of the lights on in the rest of the apartment. We creep down the hall to my room, where slowly, I open the door. Then I switch on the light, because otherwise, we won't be able to see anything. Plus, I forgot to clean my room, and I don't want anyone to break their neck.

Unfortunately, when I turn on the light, I see something else I forgot to do.

I forgot to take down my drawings.

A week ago, I taped everything I did over the summer up on the wall to see if I had gotten any better. It's not something I'd want anyone seeing anyway—even Sari—but what makes it worse is that almost every single drawing is of *Hollow Planet*.

Hollow Planet is this series of sci-fi books about a world inhabited by people known as the Exalteds. The Hollow Planet is a perfect world, there's no crime or violence, and nobody there is ugly or poor or stupid. But part of the reason the Hollow Planet is perfect is that its leaders have exiled all the criminals, thieves, and undesirables to the off-world of Prolus. The books are about the wars between the two groups.

I am obsessed with *Hollow Planet*. Sari is totally not.

I say, "Don't look at those, they're bad."

Sari doesn't listen. In fact, she goes right up to look at them. I cringe. So, I'm ridiculously fixated. It's not something everyone needs to know.

I pretend to be doing something else while Sari checks out a picture of a woman with wild flame hair, wielding a sword above her head. Queen Rana, leader of the Undesirables. At least, as I envision her. Then Sari peers at the drawing next to it and grins. "Who's Tusk Boy?"

I can tell from her face, she thinks the whole thing is ridiculous.

"Forget it, it's dumb. Let's do the Book."

That gets her away from the drawings. Raising her fists, Sari exclaims, "Fetch the Book!"

Intensely relieved, I go under my bed, where I keep the Book in a special box. Sari drags an old round rug to the middle of the room and settles down, cross-legged, on one side of it.

I sit down opposite her. "What are you going to ask it?"

"About this year. What's going to happen this year."

Now the Book, in case you were wondering, is nothing powerfully mystical or deep. It's just a paperback of *David Copperfield,* which Sari and I read last year in English. We've decided it has the power to tell the future.

We do have a reason for this. One day last year, we were studying for a test on *David Copperfield* and Sari was all worried she wouldn't pass—basically because she hadn't read any of it.

Finally, I said, "Let's ask the book."

Sari looked at me like, *Yes, she has finally lost her mind.* "Ask the book?"

"Yeah. Who would know better if you're going to pass a test on *David Copperfield* than Charles Dickens?"

So half joking, we held up the book and asked it if Sari would pass. Then I opened it, and without looking, Sari placed a finger on the page.

For a second, we stood, nervously not looking at the page and feeling kind of stupid. Then I peeked at the sentence under Sari's finger:

"And be happy," responded Dora.

"That means I pass?" said Sari.

I shrugged. "I guess."

And when she did pass—even though she spent more time worrying than studying—we decided to consult the Book on all matters of importance.

Sari is really into the Book. In some ways, even more than I am. It's been right a few times; it's been wrong a lot, too. But once she's found something to believe in, Sari doesn't let go. Fate, destiny, what's "meant to be"—she believes in all that stuff.

I lift the Book between us, cover closed. I say to Sari, "Will you speak the words?"

Sari closes her eyes. "Tell us, O Book, how does the future look?"

I wait. "Do you want to do it?"

Sari shakes her head. "No, you."

I open it, point, and read out loud. "'Anxious to be gone.'"

Sari winces. "Ouch."

It's dumb, but I can't help wondering: Is that my future or Sari's? Or both?

I want it to at least be both.

I hand her the Book. "You go."

Sari nods. Closing my eyes, I chant, "Tell us, O Book, how does the future look?"

Sari opens and points. She points very fast, her finger landing so hard on the page, I'm afraid she'll tear it.

"What does it say?"

Sari reads, "'A new one.'" She brightens up. "That's pretty good."

I'm jealous. The stupid Book has given Sari a better reading than me.

I take the Book from her. "Yeah, but it's referring to Mr. Murdstone. As David's new father.'"

"So?"

"So, Murdstone's evil."

Sari rolls her eyes. "In the book, so what?"

"Could be a warning."

Sari snorts. "It's not a *warning*. It means something new. Like new opportunities or love or—"

I interrupt. "Well, if it's a guy, he's a jerk."

I can tell from Sari's face I should give it up. I know I'm being a little creepy, but still. You can't take half the fortune and not the other half. You have to deal with the whole thing.

The thing with Sari is, she hears what she wants to hear sometimes.

Still, it's just a stupid game.

So why are Sari and I all annoyed and not saying anything?

Then she says, "Why don't you go again? Maybe it wasn't warmed up yet."

I want to say no. Rules are rules, and I had my go. But then I feel all panicky, like the Book does have power, and somehow, the difference in what it told me and what it told Sari is important. I want Sari and me to have the same year. Not the same things happening to us, but . . . I don't know.

I want us to feel the same way about things. Not her all excited, and me "Anxious to be gone."

Going again is probably cheating.

But I can't stand how it feels between me and Sari right now.

I'm about to pick up the Book when there's a knock on the door. Hiding the Book under the bed, I yell, "Come in," and my mom opens the door and sticks her head in.

Sari waves. "Hi, Mrs. Horvath."

"Hi, Sari." She smiles at me. "Don't worry, I'm not going to interrupt. I just want to tell you, spare towels and pillows are in the linen closet, okay? Now I'll get out of your way."

"Say hi to Dad," I say as Mom closes the door. For a second afterward, Sari and I just sit there. It's like a spell's been broken, and we're not sure what to do.

Finally, Sari says, "So, go ahead. Do it again."

I look over at the Book. "No. I think it tells you what it tells you, and you have to accept it."

Sari nods. Then she grins. "You know what? It's just a dumb book."

After that, we put the Book away and discuss the following issues: Will being a freshman suck? (Yes.) How much will it suck? (A lot.) Will we ever make it to sophomore year, or will we be the first people at Eldridge never to leave ninth grade? Sari says if she doesn't make it out of ninth grade, I can't leave either. And vice versa—if I fail absolutely everything, she'll stay behind with me.

For a second, I imagine myself as a 102-year-old freshman. This is entirely possible. It could very well take me eighty-eight years to understand algebra.

Around midnight, my mom knocks on the door and says, "Good night, girls," in this way that means: *lights off.* I unfold my futon chair and drag my sleeping bag out of the closet for Sari. She changes into a T-shirt of mine that has a big dog on the front, then settles right in, lying back with a sigh. I go to turn off the light, then get into my bed.

For a second, I can't see anything. Then I pull the blinds open so the moonlight comes in, and Sari's there, staring up at the ceiling like she's thinking about something really serious.

"Sar?"

"Yeah?"

"If you could pick one thing not to happen this year, what would it be?"

"Um . . . that I don't completely flunk out. What about you?"

I flop on my back and concentrate. Into the dark, I whisper, "That I don't fall prey to the evil forces of Eldridge." I say "evil" in a way that makes Sari laugh.

Then, for a long time, we don't say anything.

I think about the day. It was a good Last Day of Freedom. Even if it didn't end perfectly. I wish my picture of Sari had been good enough to give to her.

"Sar?"

"Yeah?"

"What's the thing you want to happen most?"

Sari's quiet for a while. "I don't want to say."

"Come on."

"No, it's . . . I can't explain it. It's too big. Forget it. What about you?"

"No way, I'm not saying if you're not."

"Jess . . ."

"Nuh-uh. That's it, time for sleep."

As I listen to Sari turn over, the rustle of the sleeping bag, I wonder what I would have said if Sari had said what she wanted. In the dark and quiet, I imagine I'm free to have anything I want. In my head, I hear . . .

To draw. Draw better. Have people like what I do.

Hang with Sari.

Not be around people I can't stand.

Then I think, *Forget having people like what I do.* That shouldn't be important. Art isn't about being liked. It's about being . . .

Being free.

But I don't see how you're free at school.

Then I hear Sari whisper, "Jess?"

"Hmm?"

"What do you think will really happen?"

"This year?"

"Yeah."

I think for a very long time. But the future is too big. It's like when I sit on the beach and try to draw the ocean. I can't get my eyes around it, and I always end up with a straight, flat line that doesn't look like anything.

"I don't know."

"Me either."

After what feels like a long, long time, I whisper, "Good night."

For a long time, there's just silence. For a second, I wonder if Sari's asleep.

Then I hear her say good night back, and I feel like this year will be okay.

No matter what.

2

Rana stood before the gates of the Great Palace. She knew it to be a place of cruelty—the hallowed space where the Exalteds held their festivals of humiliation. Inside the future was pain, torture, even death. At least, she smiled to herself, for them.

—Hollow Planet: Thorvald's Hammer

It's Sunday night. All day, Sari and I have been on the phone. After the last call, my mom said that was it, no more phone calls. I told her my mental state was fragile and I needed support. She said she didn't care, she just wanted her phone back.

I wonder if during the French Revolution, aristocrats headed to the guillotine felt as nervous as I do. The fact is, being guillotined only takes a second. Whereas freshman year lasts much, much longer.

Guess what wakes me up the next morning?

Alarm clock? Panic? My mom pounding on the

door, yelling, *"And I mean NOW?"* All good answers. Just not mine.

Every morning, I wake up to the sound of the crazy scrabbling of feet at my door followed by thirty-five pounds of dog hurtling itself at my head.

It's probably enough to make some people faint. But only if you're squeamish about slobber.

"Nobo" is short for "Nobody." He's a hairy little mess of a dog, and if you think my mother hasn't wondered how it is that dogs and their owners always end up looking alike, well, she has. We got him from the pound. The minute I saw him all hunched and miserable in a cage, I said, "That's my dog."

Nobody may seem like a cruel name, but it suits him. I named him that because when I got him, he looked like he had had nobody for a long time. Now he has me, and I have him, and if he knows his name sounds strange to some people, he doesn't let it bother him.

As I brush my teeth, I have the ghastly realization that I will be among my peers in one hour.

Nobo looks up at me and wags his tail. He cocks his head, like, *How come you look like you're going to puke?*

I dash down the hall, hoping to make a clean escape. Somehow, it feels important to get out of the house and on my way before my parents can turn it into a whole big production. *She's All Grown Up,* starring Jess Horvath, or something revolting like that.

But no such luck. My parents are having breakfast in the kitchen, which is just off the front-door hallway. They've heard me coming a mile away, and by the time

I'm at the door, they're both smiling at me from the table, ready to pounce.

"Well, I'm gone," I tell them.

"You feel ready?" my mom asks.

"I don't think so."

My dad examines me for a moment. In this solemn voice, he says, "I predict a year full of fulfilled potential and sustained excellence."

Then he gets up and hugs me. My dad does have a very good way of giving hugs, like he knows you're too old for that kind of thing, but he's going to hug you anyway, just because he's a big goof and he feels like it.

My mom sneaks one in too.

To get to my school, I have to take the crosstown bus through the park. I actually don't mind. It's a good way to get your head together before Eldridge rips it apart.

On the bus, I try to come up with the Worst-Case Scenario and the Best-Case Scenario for this year.

Worse-Case Scenario

- My college advisor says I am unfit for college. She advises me to get a job at McDonald's instead.

- Sari and I have no classes together.

- I get Madame Balmain instead of Madame Beauvoir for intermediate French. Madame Beauvoir est très gentile and shows Truffaut movies in class. Madame Balmain est une vache.

- I have gym first period. I have gym any period.

— Something really interesting happens to
Sari and nothing whatsoever happens to me.

Best-Case Scenario
None of the above happens.

I don't think that's too much to ask.

Actually, what I'm still hoping for is that certain people
in my class have moved, transferred, or fallen off the
face of the earth. But that probably *is* too much to ask.

Then the bus turns a corner, and here I am.

Eldridge Alternative, folks. Everybody out.

I've been going to Eldridge since the first grade, so
Eldridge High isn't totally alien territory. In fact, I've
been coming to this building ever since junior high. It's
a brick building that was probably once very cool before
they built a million ugly extensions onto it. We're just
a block away from the park, which has this old stone
wall, and when it's nice, people hang out there. Not
that I ever have—the wall is strictly the territory of the
cool and the privileged.

What else can I tell you about Eldridge Alternative?
Well, for one thing, we're all very creative. Some of us are
rich, and a lot of us don't take tests well. Otherwise, our
parents would have put us into a better private school
or one of those public schools where they're always win-
ning science prizes.

A lot of the teachers are into "relating." They don't

yell, they talk. They don't punish, they find out what's going on. They want us to feel that they're one of us—like that's such a great thing to be.

When I reach the entrance to the school, I can see a lot of my fellow freshmen hanging out on the street. The rest of the school won't turn up until noon, because the first part of the day is reserved for Freshman Orientation. Which means we'll get a big talk on how IMPORTANT everything is now. How our grades are IMPORTANT, how our test scores are IMPORTANT, how our school record is IMPORTANT. Then we sign up for classes. Then we make appointments with the school college advisor to plan out the next four years of our lives so we can get into a great school that looks good on Eldridge's record. That, I think, is what's most IMPORTANT to Eldridge.

Looking at the crowd outside, I can see all these people I sort of know and sort of don't. I have no idea if I say hi to them they will say hi back. In the end, I decide to play it safe: say nothing. Instead, I just put my head down and charge up the stairs, like some criminal going up the courtroom steps in a movie.

Sari and I have agreed to meet by the third-floor bathroom. My mission is to reach the third floor without running into anyone who will make me barf upon encounter.

By which I mean the Prada Mafia.

The Prada Mafia is the clique of five or six girls whose goal in life is to wear nothing but Prada. Not really up there with ending world hunger or finding the cure for cancer. They are all very rich, and their combined IQ is roughly equivalent to that of a kumquat. They think they rule our class—and unfortunately, they do.

Their leader is this chick named Erica Trager. I hate Erica Trager. Not the way I kind of hate most people at school, but deeply, personally *hate*. She never eats—it's like a sin. Her vocabulary is limited to, "My daddy bought me" (fill in the blank with designer clothes, cell phones, computers, ski trips, you name it). And she's nasty. The kind of person who has friends just to put them down. "Are you sure you should *eat* that?" she says to her lamebrained sorority sisters. "Were we a little color blind when we got dressed this morning?" She's the kind of person who gives females a bad name, if you know what I mean.

No sign of Erica or the Prada Mafia, so it seems safe to proceed to the third floor. Dash up the stairs. Pause. Check that the coast is clear through the glass window in the door. (*No sign of Prada, chief. You're good to go.*) Push door open and race to the lockers by the third-floor girls' bathroom. Slump against locker, try to look like I have been there for hours and am already bored.

Now I'm seeing a lot of people I know. I nod to Liza Kleinberg, who's our resident poet. I smile a little bit at Nicky Patterson and Zoe Haas. Nicky's really tall and thin and has this quiet voice. Zoe is short and fat and has a very loud voice. They've been best friends for as long as I can remember. Sari says Nicky is gay, but I don't see how she knows.

It's so weird—it's only been three months since I saw all these guys, and they feel like total strangers. I wonder how I seem to them.

Probably not all that important.

If you want to know where I fall on the social status scale, just look down. Way down. When you get to the level of Repugnant and Reviled, start looking up again till you get to Weird and Ignored. That's me. My parents don't like to hear this, but it's a fact of life at Eldridge that if you have half a brain, those who are popular will make your life miserable. If you think there's more to life than money and designer clothes, they will torture you. Needless to say, a fanatical sci-fi nerd is not their idea of cool.

Still, even I am not uncool enough to be pleased that the first person to speak to me is Danny Oriel.

It's not that I don't like Danny. I do. It's just that he's . . . embarrassing. He thinks we're friends, and I keep wanting to tell him, *We're not. I'm just one of the few people on the planet who will speak to you.*

Hollow Planet is the reason why Danny thinks we're friends. Last year, he caught me reading volume four of *Hollow Planet* in hardcover, and he said, "They're making a movie, you know." And I said, "It'll suck." And he said, "Yeah, Hollywood ruins everything good."

And that was kind of that. See, Danny is the only other person at school who's as big a *Hollow Planet* freak as I am—and who will *admit* it. He never pretends to be above it. That is one thing I can say about him: He's honest that way. But frankly, he should be, because *Hollow Planet* is his entire existence.

For example, instead of saying hello to me like a normal person, the first thing he says is, "Only two hundred and fifty-three more days until *Hollow Planet: The Film* comes out."

I say, "You don't know when it's coming out, Danny. They haven't set a release date yet."

He shakes his head. "No. I read it on HolPlan.com. Some guy has a brother who works in the mail room in the studio where they're making it, and he says . . ."

If honesty is a nice thing about Danny, boringness is definitely a big drawback. He can just go on and on and on until you want to smack him. Lately, I've been trying to figure out what makes a person weird and what makes them a nerd. The difference? Nerds talk too much.

In fact, he's such a gumball, I decide to play with his mind a little.

"Well, here's what I heard. They're killing off Thor."

Danny's mouth falls open. "No way. Where'd you hear that?"

"Cinescape."

"It's gotta be wrong."

I shake my head. "Nope. Totally confirmed."

"Oh, man." Danny slaps his fist into his palm. "The movie's gonna *suck.*"

For the record, Danny is unable to say the word "suck" with any authority. Same with "Oh, man."

I nod sadly. "Yep, I know."

Just then, I see Sari coming through the crowd. She's smiling and waving at me. But when she sees Danny, she gets this look like she's one of those chicks in a horror movie and the psycho killer has jumped out at her with a huge knife.

Slowly, like she's creeping up to zap Danny with bug spray, she approaches, then gives me a huge hug. "Hey . . ."

The she gives Danny a fast smile. "Hi."

"Oh, hey, Sari." Danny smiles back, then looks down at his feet. Sari has that effect on boys. Especially Nerdboy.

Sari asks Danny how his summer was. He starts telling her. (I can sum it up for you in a single word: "boring.") Sari's nodding and smiling. But then she starts giving me this desperate look, like, *I am not going to be seen hanging out with Danny Oriel on the first day of school. Do something NOW.*

Immediately, I say, "I have to go to the bathroom."

"Right," says Sari. "Me too."

Saying, "Sorry, Danny, see you later, Danny," we disappear into the girls' room. As I close the door, Sari slumps against the wall and shudders. "Phew. I mean, I'm sorry, but . . . creepy Geekboy alert."

I say, "He's harmless."

"Exactly." Sari gives me a last shudder, then starts checking herself out in the mirror. We have to go to orientation in a few minutes. God forbid she walk in looking less than fabulous.

I have no interest in looking fabulous, so I decide to check out the graffiti on the bathroom wall. The place is like Gossip Central. Check out the stalls, and you'll find out anything you want to know about Eldridge Alternative.

Even though the janitors have tried really hard to wash the old messages off over the summer, you can still see a few:

Thea ♥ David BIG TIME!

Does anyone think Mr. Kenin smells, or is it just me? (Right near this: *God yes!* and *No, it's just you.*)

In need of weed? Go to Reed.

It's also an excellent place to get dirt on teachers—who's okay and who blows. There's a lot about Mr. Barry, one of the English teachers, a *Hey, I'm one of you* type of guy. Opinion is definitely split on Barry:

> *Barry rules!*
>> *Barry sucks!*
>>> *Barry inhales.*

I'm just checking out what's left of last year's messages when the door opens and my worst nightmare comes true. We are besieged by the Prada Mafia.

Erica Trager and her cronies take over the bathroom like they own it. (Well, don't they own everything? Of course. Mummy and Daddy buy it for them.) Me they totally ignore. I'm not even worth their contempt. But they all stop and sneer when they see Sari.

It's funny—you might think the Prada Mafia would be nicer to Sari. I mean, she at least gets the whole clothes-and-guys thing. But for some reason, ever since last year, they've been particularly nasty to her.

Here's what I think it's about: hotness. Hotness matters. Everyone tries to tell you it doesn't, but it does. It's like money. Some people have it, some people don't. Sari is hot. And a lot of girls don't like her because of it. Not if they have pretensions to hotness themselves. If you think you are hot but are in fact not hot, Sari lets you know it. Not that she ever says anything. She just kind of shows you what it's about.

People like the Prada Mafia think she's slutty. But they don't know anything about her.

I, of course, have no pretensions to hotness, so I have nothing to fear from Sari. Which is why I know that she's nice and funny and a little crazy, and very few other people do.

Erica and her little crew just kind of hang back, making it clear they won't touch a thing until we vacate the premises with our unclean selves. Which we do. As we go, Sari gives them this look, like, *Oh, my God, something SMELLS.*

When we're outside, she says, "Hate them."

And I say, "Destroy them."

I glance back toward the bathroom. I wish I'd had the guts to do something. Spray them or something. Erica is such a cockroach. She definitely deserves to get zapped with Raid.

We head to the Little Eldridge Theater for the dreaded orientation. Which is exactly as obnoxious as I thought it would be. At the end of it, Peter McElroy, our college admissions counselor, gets up onstage. He is here to enlighten us about freshman year. Here is what he has to say:

Get all A's . . .

Score 1600 on your SATs . . .

Sign up for a hundred extracurricular activities . . .

Get into Harvard, and you'll be just fine . . .

Don't, and you'll be dog doo.

I mean, that's not exactly what McElroy says. He puts in a lot of blah-blah about meaningful experiences and discovering yourself and making friends that last a lifetime, but what it really boils down to is: Don't screw up. Don't make us look bad.

I glance over at Sari, who's looking about as pukey as I feel.

I want to raise my hand and ask: *What if we can't do any of these things? What if we're good at some things but not so fabulous at others? What if I have to throw up in the middle of my SATs? What if we're just sort of . . . average?*

Will you hunt us down and have us killed?

Immediately after orientation, we have to rush around like crazy people to sign up for classes. I'm so nuts, I have no idea what I'm doing, just that I beg for art instead of chorus and tell Madame Beauvoir that I really, really hope I get into her intermediate French class. She smiles and tells me a lot of people have said the exact same thing.

Tomorrow, we'll get a printed schedule, telling us what classes we got. *Just one class with Sari,* I think. *That's all I ask. That, and no classes with the Prada Mafia.*

At lunch, Sari keeps saying over and over, "I can't do this."

I say, "Me neither."

After lunch, the rest of the high school starts to arrive. Suddenly, the halls are crowded, and the stairs are so full of people, it's hard to get up and down. The sophomores, juniors, seniors have taken over. They're all yakking and slapping hands. You try to get past them, and forget it; no way do they move for some measly freshman. They all look like they know what they're doing, like they've been here before and it's no big thing.

As Sari and I trudge upstairs for first-day assembly, I wonder if I will look like that next year.

I doubt it.

But when we finally make it into the auditorium, and the entire high school is there in one big crowd, I have to admit, I feel a little excited in a corny way. Everyone is up and walking around, finding friends to sit with or pretending to be so into reading something that they don't care that they're sitting alone. Sari and I find a place at the back of the auditorium. It's Sari's idea, and it's smart. A lot of our classmates have sat right up front, and they look like eager-beaver losers.

From the back, we can watch as people come in. Sari keeps nudging me, saying things like, "There's Eric, our resident pot dealer." Or, "Oh, my God, she's still a stick," about Allison Bell, who was out of school last year because she was in the hospital for anorexia. Or, "Oh, gag. Daisy Fisher," who volunteers whenever they need someone to run something. Bake sales, canned food drives, school raffles . . . you just know Daisy's going to be out there going, *Buy, buy, buy. It's all for Eldridge!*

Things are getting really hysterical now. Every two seconds, the gym doors swing open and there are huge cheers. The seniors have arrived, all pumped for the first day of their last year. A crowd is starting to form at the doors, mostly the elite crew—the soccer guys and their girlfriends. Every time one of them comes in, the rest of them hold out their hands, and the new arrival runs through, slapping hands like some jerk at the Super Bowl.

You just know they wouldn't be doing it if no one were here to watch them. It's totally about, *Look how great we are, how amazing and above you.* Of course, they're completely blocking the door, so everyone else has to squeeze through the crowd and run for a seat.

They're all whooping and cheering like fools. I say, "Would someone please hose them down?"

But Sari isn't listening. She's staring at the crowd, eyes shining, not wanting to miss a thing. Her mouth's open, like she's ready to call out to someone; she's up on her toes, like she wants to run right over there.

I'm about to say something else when she jumps and starts craning to see into the crowd. Startled, I look where she's looking. At first, I don't get it. Then I see David Cole.

He's laughing, as usual. He's one of those people who's always laughing—usually at someone. A billion people rush forward, all pounding his back, slapping his hand. Somehow, just by coming in, he's made everything about him, like we're all here to welcome him or something.

"Oh, my God, how hot is he?" Sari whispers.

I roll my eyes. "Sari, give it up."

But she's still staring at him. Well, she can stare all she wants, but I guess she's not noticing that right next to David is his girlfriend, Thea Melendez. And if Sari thinks she's messing with that, she's dreaming.

David and Thea are the official Eldridge couple. They started going out last year when they were juniors. David was this really out-of-control guy who was always getting kicked out of class for screwing up and mouthing off. According to some people, he was on the verge of being expelled.

So, needless to say, everyone was shocked when he started dating Thea, who is Miss Perfect Popular.

Nobody thought it would last. But it has. For real. Some people just "go out." But David and Thea are, like, in love. Whatever that means.

I can definitely see why Sari thinks David's hot. A lot of people do. He's got this very dark hair, and he's lean because he's a soccer freak. He's sarcastic and self-confident. But Sari can forget it. Frankly she has a better chance of going out with Bailey Watts.

Now the administrators start filing onto the dais, to many hoots from the crowd. But there's no sign of our fearless leader, Jeannie Carsalot, also known as Gee-She-Farts-a-Lot. At any other school, Jeannie Carsalot would be called a principal. Here, she calls herself director of education. Don't ask me why.

Finally, Maisie Sheridan, the assistant director of education, gets up onstage. Crazy Maisie is, like, six feet tall and weighs absolutely nothing, so she looks like this huge, nervous noodle.

She starts banging on the microphone and asks us all to shut up. She says: "People"—I hate it when people call you "people"; it's like they're trying to stop themselves from calling you something else—"People, it's time to settle down. Okay? Okay, people?"

Nobody settles down.

"People? Okay? Can we . . . Can we just listen up?"

Nobody listens up.

Maisie just stands there like she would like to hurl the microphone at us.

Some of the seniors start howling. Maisie gets out a few more "Okay"s and "All right"s. Then she gives up and hands us over to Jeannie Farts-a-Lot.

Jeannie Farts-a-Lot is roughly the size of a small planet. She walks right up to the microphone, grabs it, and yells, "HI!"

You swear the walls shake. Like the gym floor is just going to give way. But for some crazy reason, we all yell, "HI!" right back at her.

"I can tell we're feeling good to be here," says Jeannie Farts-a-Lot.

And I guess we are, because we are all cheering.

Then, before I know it, it's 3:30 and it's all over. My first official day of high school is over.

And I lived through it and everything.

The next day, I get my class schedule. I open it, and there it is—my life on a computer printout.

```
Name: Horvath, Jesse
Grade: Nine

MONDAY
8:30-9:00 Homeroom
9:10-10:00 Gym (D. Melnick)
10:15-11:00 Intermediate French
    (G. Balmain) [I have Madame Balmain!
    Argh!]
11:15-12:00 Biology (E. Feiffer)
1:15-2:30 Algebra (B. McGuiness)
2:45-3:30 20th Century European
    History (A. Burgess)

TUESDAY
8:30-9:00 Homeroom
9:10-10:00 Algebra (B. McGuiness)
10:15-11:00 English Literature
    (H. Barry)
11:15-12:00 Intermediate French
    (G. Balmain)
```

```
1:15-2:30 Biology (E. Feiffer)
2:45-3:30 Art (S. Rothstein)
```

WEDNESDAY
```
8:30-9:00 Homeroom
9:10-10:00 Gym (D. Melnick)
10:15-11:00 English Literature
    (H. Barry)
11:15-12:00 Art (S. Rothstein)
1:15-2:30 20th Century European
    History (A. Burgess)
2:45-3:30 Biology (E. Feiffer)
```

THURSDAY
```
8:30-9:00 Homeroom
9:10-10:00 Intermediate French
    (G. Balmain) [Argh, argh!]
10:15-11:00 English Literature
    (H. Barry)
11:15-12:00 Gym (D. Melnick)
1:15-2:30 Study Period
2:45-3:30 Algebra (B. McGuiness)
```

FRIDAY
```
8:30-9:00 Homeroom
9:10-10:00 Intermediate French
    (G. Balmain) [Argh, argh, argh!]
10:15-11:00 Gym (D. Melnick)
11:15-12:00 Art (S. Rothstein)
1:15-2:30 20th Century European
    History (A. Burgess)
2:45-3:30 Biology (E. Feiffer)
```

I can't believe this. I will never survive. Gym for first period—which only proves that Sari is right: There is no God—and when not gym, French! What kind of universe expects me to conjugate French verbs at 9:00 in the morning? And for English, I have Mr. Barry, who's supposed to give new meaning to the word "creepazoid," and for art, Stella Rothstein, who's probably a big airhead who thinks everything should be "pretty."

And the only class—the *only* class—I have with Sari is English.

Well, so much for awesome. This year has definitely taken a turn for the horrific.

3

The actions of the Verduli were inexplicable. They kept their own counsel, made their own rules. There was a saying: "To have a Verdul as your ally is to have the enemy at your back."

—*Hollow Planet: The Darkening Storm*

HALLOWEEN DANCE

frightfully fun!   Scary Good Time!

Thrills! Chills! (But Hopefully No Spills!)

"Whoa," I say to Sari. "Thrills and chills. Is that legal?"

"Look." Sari points to a sign-up sheet. "You too can be a part of it all. *'Boo! We need you!'* Let's see. We have the Food Committee . . ."

"Gummi worms and popcorn balls."

"Music Committee."

"Truly horrifying."

"Decorations Committee."

"Ooh, ooh. Black and orange twisted crepe paper and balloons."

It's weird what you can get used to. I've been a freshman for only a month, and already high school is no big deal.

On my first real day of classes, every teacher told me the same thing: that I would work harder in their class than in all my other classes.

How I'm supposed to work harder in every class than in all my other classes, I don't know. That night, I asked my mother if it was okay if I became a janitor.

I look at the lame party sign. Frankly, the whole thing just confirms my opinion that Halloween hasn't been any good since I stopped trick-or-treating.

I say, "Clearly, what we must do is bag the whole thing, go to my house, and rent truly disgusting videos."

Sari says, "Definitely."

I take a pencil out of my bag and start signing the volunteer sheets: Eugenia Flatulence. Horatio Fecal-matter. I'm trying to decide if Ana L. Retentiv is worth it when Sari says, "Look."

I look. I don't see.

"Thea Melendez signed up for decorations."

I look at the sign-up sheet. There's Thea's name all right. But I don't see anything amazing about it. Thea's always doing things like that. Sometimes she even gets Lord God David Cole to help her, even though he obviously thinks stuff like that is for losers.

I glance at my watch. "Sari, we are seriously late for English."

Sari's still looking at the stupid sign-up sheet.

Don't ask me why. Sometimes I can't figure Sari out.

When classes started, I thought if I had to have Sari in just one class, I'd want it to be English, because Mr. Barry is definitely not someone you want to face alone.

I thought wrong.

Remember the raging bathroom debate on Mr. Barry? How everybody was fighting about whether Barry rules or Barry sucks? Well, I'm definitely in the Barry sucks camp.

Sari thinks he's kind of cool.

But that's only because Mr. Barry thinks Sari is *way* cool.

Every time she comes to class, he stands up and says, "Hi, Sari," in this moronic voice. She never raises her hand, but he's always asking her, "What do you think, Sari?" And when she says, "I have no idea," he says, "How come? Didn't do the reading?" And all Sari has to say is, "I did the reading," and he lets her off the hook.

Yet another advantage of hotness.

For the record, and in case you care, Mr. Barry is not hot.

Mr. Barry is very tall and very skinny, with this goofy way of talking that makes him sound like he's our age instead of what he is—which is decrepit. The very irritating thing about Mr. Barry is that he flirts like a madman, but he still wants you to think that he's a

Good Guy. That he's not a Creep. And I'm sorry, but when you laugh, and touch, and give compliments the way he gives compliments ("That's a great sweater, Sari"), I don't care how "nice" you are; you've earned your place in the Creep Pantheon.

We're reading *Romeo and Juliet,* which is vomitous. As far as I'm concerned, the sooner these two dippy schmoes off themselves, the better. Then we can move on to *Macbeth,* which at least has witches and a few decent murders.

Barry's got us reading the whole play aloud. This, he says, gives us the opportunity to fully appreciate the greatness of the verse. This, *I* think, gives him a chance to goof off and not do a lot, except say, "Okay, guys, what's Romeo feeling here?"

We're up to the party scene where Romeo and Juliet first meet. Naturally, Mr. Barry calls on Sari to play Juliet.

Unfortunately for Sari, he asks Danny Oriel to read Romeo.

I take *Hollow Planet* out and slide it onto my lap, like I'm reading along. I've seen the movie. I know what happens. They fall in love. They get married. They die. End of story.

Here's what I hate about *Romeo and Juliet:* all the secrets. Nobody says what they should when they should to the person they should say it to. Like in this scene, Romeo's wearing a mask, so Juliet doesn't figure out who he is until it's too late. And Romeo doesn't just tell Mercutio why he doesn't want him fighting with Tybalt, never says, *Wait, stop, I'm in love with his cousin.*

No, he lets Mercutio think he's just a big fat wuss—which he is—and Mercutio and Tybalt end up dead. And the Nurse knows she should give a heads-up to Juliet's mom and dad, but . . . she doesn't. You know? It's all missing letters and hidden identity and, *Oh, oops, darling, I'm not really dead, I just looked that way. But, oh, dear, now you* are *dead.*

I can't stand that stuff.

Mr. Barry is asking Sari, "So, what do you think Juliet's feeling at this party?"

I expect Sari to give her usual "I don't know." But instead, she says, "I think she's excited."

Sari saying the word "excited" really does something for Barry. Leaning forward, he says, "Yeah, what's she excited about?"

"Like, maybe finally something will happen to her. Like, she's not a little girl anymore."

"And something does happen, right?"

Sari gives him a look like, *Have you read this play?* and says, "Well, yeah, she meets Romeo."

"And falls in love."

"Right."

"Still think she's a little girl?"

Sari doesn't answer right away, so Danny jumps in: "I think if you're just kissing with your hands, yeah, you're still pretty immature."

Sari snorts. "Yeah, like you would know, you mad lover, you."

Then Barry asks us what it means that Romeo is wearing a mask, a question no one knows the answer to. We all go, "Um" for a long time, and then class is over.

As we leave, Barry yells after us, "Think about it for next time—masks, mistaken identities, preconceived notions . . ."

Out in the hall, I say to Sari, "God, I can't wait till we're done with this play."

Sari shrugs. "It's a lot better than *Great Expectations*."

I absolutely do not agree. At least *Great Expectations* had the rats in the wedding cake. And Miss Havisham spontaneously combusting.

A few days later, as we're walking to class, I ask Sari which videos she thinks we should rent on Halloween. She gives me a totally blank look.

"For our Halloween extravaganza."

"Oh."

"I was thinking first a classic, like *Friday the 13th*. Then something new. And maybe something goofy, like *Scream*."

Sari frowns. "Yeah . . ."

She's not really listening, I can tell. For some reason, she keeps glancing down the hall.

"It doesn't have to be *Friday the 13th*. It could be—"

But then Sari interrupts. "I got to go. I'm going to be late."

"Okay."

I watch her run down the hall to her class. Lots of kids are going in. Then a guy who's passing by holds the door open for Sari.

David Cole.

Sari smiles as she goes in.

David smiles back.

And then they're both gone. For a second, I watch the space where they were. And then I realize *I'm* late and run to art class.

One thing that is absolutely better about high school is the art room. In junior high, all we had was this dark, dinky room in the basement. And all they gave us was a lot of old clay, dried-up paints, and brushes that were really stiff.

But over the summer, the school built this new art room on the top floor of the building. It's enormous, with windows all around, so there's tons of light. You can see out over the tops of the buildings, look up at the sky. The tables are high, and you sit on tall stools that let your legs swing free and feel like you're sitting up in a tree.

I love the art room. It's the one place in the whole school that's quiet. The one place I feel like I can breathe.

Because I'm late, when I open the door, everyone looks up, including Stella Rothstein, who smiles. "Hi, Jess. Come on in."

I scramble up on a stool, open up my sketch pad.

It's funny—when I'm in the art room, I forget I'm at Eldridge.

All that week, I wait for Sari to say whether or not she likes my movie choices. I need to know, because she's pretty picky about movies. But she doesn't bring it up.

The week after that, we are in the gym. I call the gym the Hall of Happy Thought. Once a month, we have community awareness assemblies, in which grades nine through twelve are exposed to something inspiring and life affirming. A documentary on the homeless. A slide show on the Middle East. Music that sounds like a sick cat. That kind of thing.

Sari swears she's going to start cutting every single assembly and go smoke on the park wall. This is definitely the fashionable thing to do, but frankly, I'm too chicken. Also, I don't know. It doesn't seem right to skip out for a cig so you don't have to see starving kids. Besides, my dad has promised me that if I ever start smoking, he'll rip my lungs out for free.

This assembly is so we can hear the speeches from people running for the president of student government. Nobody good ever runs for these things. Like this year, Daisy Fisher is running. She's up there now, her stupid speech in her hands, trying not to look down too much while she talks so she can flash us this big cheesy smile that's supposed to look sincere.

Her opponent is Eric Reed. A lot of people say they're going to vote for him. I am definitely going to vote for him. Anybody but Dippy Daisy.

In the middle of some endless blah-blah about cleaner bathrooms, Daisy drops her speech. While she kneels down to get it, I write in my notebook and show it to Sari: *I'm going to go reserve videos this afternoon. Want to come?*

I have to nudge her to get her to look at it. She frowns and kind of shakes her head.

Daisy's trying to find the place where she left off, so I whisper, "Well, is what I said okay?"

"I don't remember."

"Well, we should decide, because all the good ones will be reserved otherwise."

Then Daisy starts up again, so we have to be quiet. Then she finishes, and people go clap, clap, clap.

Now it's Eric's turn to make his speech. It is three words long. It is . . .

"Vote for Reed!"

Everyone bursts into cheers, and Eric stalks around the stage, pumping his fists in the air. The whole place is chanting, "Reed! Reed! Reed!"

Daisy Fisher looks like she's going to cry. I'm chanting "Reed!" too, but for a second, I feel a little sorry for her.

I glance over at Sari. She is not chanting "Reed!" She's just staring off into space—something she's doing a lot of these days. I feel like asking, *What is* with *you?*

As we leave the Hall of Happy Thought to go downstairs, I say to her, "Look, what if I just go pick the movies, and then—"

Sari frowns, and I can tell she has something she both wants to say and doesn't want to say.

"What?"

"No, I'm just thinking."

"Okay, thinking what?"

We get to our lockers. Pulling her coat on, Sari says, "What if, before we do videos, we just stop by the Halloween dance?"

I make an immediate vomit noise.

"Not for a long time. Just to see what's going on."

"I know what'll be going on. Grossness and stupidity. No thank you."

Now Sari's pissed off. "Well, I might want to go."

"Well, then, *go.*"

"Good, fine. I will."

And just like that, we're not doing videos. Just like that, I'm stuck with nothing to do on Halloween, and Sari's going to this asinine dance.

And on top of everything else, we're pissed at each other.

For the rest of the day, I keep trying to figure out what happened. It's like I have two voices in my head: my Nice Self, which feels bad, and my Pissed-Off Self, which feels . . . pissed.

My Nice Self points out that I shouldn't have been surprised that Sari wants to go to the dance. She's always been more into that kind of thing than I have.

Then my Pissed-Off Self says, *Yeah, but she agreed to hang out that night.*

Sari didn't say she didn't want to hang out, says Nice Self. *She just wanted to do something different while you were hanging out. Like go to this dance.*

Well, guess what? says Pissed-Off Self. *I can't stand dances.*

Yeah, but Sari likes them.

And neither self has an answer for that one.

The next day at school, I don't see Sari all day. Which I guess means we're avoiding each other. Which is okay, because I'm not speaking to her.

And I guess she isn't speaking to me either.

I reserve the movies anyway. When I give the guy my

video card, I think, *Maybe when Sari realizes the dance is totally asinine, she'll want to come over.*

We've never had a fight before. It feels strange.

If Sari isn't speaking to me, it means she's as pissed at me for not going to the dance as I am at her for going. Which I totally don't get.

Fine, whatever. Let Sari go to the stupid Halloween dance. Let her look for whatever it is she's looking for. Who cares?

Yeah, says Nice Self. *But if you'd gone, you could have hung out with Sari like you planned.*

Oh, shut up. I think. *I'm renaming you Loser Self.*

And Loser Self is pretty much how I feel on Halloween, sitting alone in the living room, with a huge bowl of popcorn and a bag of M&M's, watching my mother run to the door every time the bell rings. I look at the three videos, trying to decide which one I want to watch first. I was so psyched to get them. Now I feel like they all suck.

There's some kind of contest on the M&M's bag. *Aha,* I think. *I shall win a million dollars, a car, and a trip to Hawaii.* I will give the car to my parents, primarily because I can't drive yet. I will refuse to share any of it with Sari. She will be miserable she was not here to win with me.

Tearing the bag open I read, "'Sorry, this bag is not a winner. Please try again.'"

I'm putting in a video when I hear the phone ring in the kitchen. I put the movie on pause and listen as my mom answers it. "Hello?"

I wait, hoping to hear, *Oh, hi, Sari. Hold on . . .*

But then my mom says, "Miriam, how are you?" and I know it's my aunt. They will be on the phone forever.

So even if Sari does call, all she'll get is a busy signal.

And guess what? She's not calling.

I flop on the couch and hit PLAY.

Stuffing a handful of popcorn in my mouth, I try to convince myself I am having a good time.

It doesn't work.

Nobo wanders in looking for popcorn. I watch as this chick races through the woods, screaming, and wonder: *A mad killer is after you, and your makeup is totally perfect. Your hair bounces perfectly, like in some creepy shampoo ad.* Of course, the camera stays on her chest the whole entire time.

My mom passes by the living room on her way back from appeasing the hordes. Hearing the screams, she stops and makes a face. "*What* are you watching?"

"*Camp Killer 2.*" My mom looks horrified. "A maniac goes after camp counselors because they work at the camp where his little sister drowned . . . *many years ago.*"

"That's grotesque." My mom comes in and sits down.

I grin. "Oh, it is."

As we watch the movie, I can tell my mom is completely grossed out. She doesn't say anything, but she keeps making these faces like she swallowed putrid phlegm. This is my mother's normal reaction to most of what I like.

Reaching for the popcorn, she says, "I thought Sari was coming over tonight."

I shrug. "She changed her mind."

"Oh." She's pretending not to be curious, but I know she is.

I really don't want to tell my mom about the dance. But I can feel her wanting to know, and so, finally, I say, "They're having this Halloween dance at school, and she wanted to go."

My mom nods. Then, supercasual, she asks, "You didn't want to go?"

"*No.*"

"How come?"

"Because I would rather eat rancid rat than go."

"Ah, hon." My mom laughs. I look away, feeling like she's laughing at me. If she didn't want to know the answer, then she shouldn't have asked.

"Can I ask why you'd rather eat rancid rat?" Her voice is gentle.

"Because . . ." I slump, dig my heels into the rug. "It's all just a big stupid game. All you do is wait around for someone to notice you so you feel like you exist."

"Are you sure? I thought they were just big parties where people, you know, danced."

Now she's teasing me. I say lightly, "Yes, I'm sure they were in 1847. But times have changed since you were a girl."

For a second, I'm scared she'll be annoyed. But instead, she laughs and hugs me. "Okay, you win," she says into my hair.

Normally, with a hug, I would sit up after a second. But for some reason, I just sort of hang out in my mom's lap for a while. We watch the rest of the movie, and I drop popcorn on the floor for Nobo, until Mom tells me to quit it, it'll make him sick.

And that's how I spend Halloween.

That night, before I go to bed, I check the answering machine. No one has called.

I guess Sari's having a good time at the dance.

4

On Monday, while I'm on the bus to school, my Nice Self and my Pissed-Off Self have another argument.

Nice Self thinks I should ask Sari how the dance was. Pissed-Off Self says: *Make her come groveling with apologies.*

I really do think Sari owes me an apology. And I don't think I should speak to her until I get it.

The only problem is, I miss her.

Sometimes during a class, if I know I'm about to pass out cold from boredom, I ask to go to the bathroom. I take my book, and I just sit there and read, until my brain wakes up again.

That's exactly what happens to me just before Madame Balmain has a chance to ask me to conjugate *venir*.

And that's how I end up hearing what I hear in the third-floor girls' bathroom.

When I get there, I've got the place to myself. Then, when I'm settled in the left-hand stall, I hear the bathroom door open and what sounds like two or three girls come in. They're all talking at once, and at first, it's kind of hard to tell who they are.

Then I peek under the stall door and see their shoes. Prada Mafia.

"God, could you believe her?"

"I just could not believe her."

Voice One is definitely Erica Trager. Voice Two is probably Michelle Burke, her dim flunky.

"I was just, like, how trashy can you be?"

"Well . . ." Big snort from Michelle. "Pretty trashy."

"Oh, yes." Erica's voice was turned all prim. "I forgot we were talking about Sari Aaronsohn."

Carefully, I lift my feet off the floor. I hope they don't notice that one door is closed.

"I mean, that *skeleton* costume she had on . . ."

"Please, you mean sprayed on."

"So slutty."

I am about to get up and say, *Who do you think you are?* when I hear Michelle say:

"And the way she was going after him."

I freeze. Who him? Which him?

"Oh, my *God*."

"Totally pathetic."

I'm dying to tell them how pathetic they are. But I

also want to find out who they're talking about. So I stay where I am, quiet and hidden.

"I mean, good *luck,* honey."

"Like he would ever look at her."

"Yeah. I mean, hello, when he's . . ."

Their voices are fading out, so I don't get to hear who this guy is and why he would never look at Sari. Lots of guys look at Sari. Why wouldn't this one?

He probably would, I think, and that's what's got Erica and Michelle so twisted.

I sit there for a long time, thinking. Is this why Sari went to the dance? Because she wanted to see this guy? Or did it happen by accident? What I mean is, is this someone she really likes?

If it is, why didn't she tell me about him?

And who is he, anyway?

Back in French class, while Madame Balmain is enlightening us about the glories of the *plus-que-parfait,* I try to think of who Mr. Him could be. It could be Craig Schaeffer. Sari had a big crush on him last year. A few weeks ago, she called him a snot, but she could have been pretending. Or maybe it's Eric Reed, who used to have this big crush on her. At least, he teased her a lot. But no way would Sari have to chase Eric Reed.

I seriously hope it's not Mr. Barry. If it's Mr. Barry, I will have to take Sari to one of those clinics where they fry your brains.

But if I'm honest, none of these guys feels like Him.

So I guess I have to wait for Sari to tell me.

That is, if she ever speaks to me again.

At lunchtime, I'm sitting in the cafeteria, reading *Hollow Planet,* when I hear, "Hi."

I look up and see Sari. She's looking nervous, but also kind of pissed off. Like if I don't say exactly the right thing, she's ready to split.

I could just look back down at my book. Not say a thing.

But Sari did make the first move.

I figure the least I can do is move over so she can sit down.

Which I do, and she does.

For a second, we just sit there. Then I decide it's better to get everything out in the open. So I ask, "How was Friday night?"

Sari shrugs. "Okay. Kind of dumb."

Then she says, "It would have been better if you'd been there."

It's weird—how one nice thing can make you forget you were ever mad at someone.

To be nice back, I say, "Maybe next time I'll come."

"Yeah?" Sari nudges me, like a dare or something.

"Yeah, maybe." Then I say, "I heard your costume was hot."

"Oh, yeah?" Sari brightens up. "Who from?"

Oops.

"Um, some girl? I overheard her in the bathroom."

"Oh." I can tell from her face that Sari is disappointed it was not Him.

I decide to push a little. "So, who else was there?"

"Nobody, really."

I'm about to ask how she could hang with nobody for

a whole dance when she says, "How were the movies?"

I smile. "Kind of dumb. Definitely would have been better if you'd been there."

So, Sari and I are back to being friends. Everything's great, right?

Right.

Only here's the thing: Sari's not saying a word about Mr. Him. A week goes by, and nothing. I listen carefully whenever she talks about a guy or even Mr. Barry, but it's not like her eyes light up or anything.

At first I figure she doesn't want to bring up anything about the dance, since we had a fight about it. But then I realize, whatever happened at the stupid dance, whoever He was, she's not going to talk about it, period.

Which I don't get. Sari always tells me everything. She's like that.

Was like that.

Is this guy so gross that she's embarrassed? Or is it just me she doesn't want to tell for some reason? Why wouldn't she tell me?

Question: How do you get someone to tell you something they don't want you to know?

One day, I say in a casual voice, "I saw Craig Schaeffer checking you out yesterday in assembly."

Now, last year, Sari would have freaked if I said that. She would have demanded to know when, where, and for how long.

Now she just says, "Oh, barf."

I say, "I thought you liked him."

Sari looks at me like I'm demented. "Yeah, *last* year."

In other words: *A zillion eons ago, when I was a mere child.*

Okay, Craig's out.

The next day, I say, "You know who's looking kind of cute this year?"

"Who?"

"Eric."

Sari frowns. "Eric?"

"Reed."

Sari shrieks, "Oh, my God, I just ate."

Scratch Eric off the list. (As an added bonus, my best friend now thinks I have hideous taste in men.)

Finally, I'm left with my least-favorite candidate, Mr. Barry. I will die if Sari likes Mr. Barry. It will be so creepy, I won't be able to stand it. I'll have to kidnap her and drag her to some deprogramming center. (Probably the same one she wants to take me to now that she thinks I think Eric Reed is cute.)

One afternoon, after English class, I work up the nerve to ask her, "So, would you do it?"

"Do what?"

"With Mr. Barry."

Sari makes a very candid and believable face, and says, "G.W." This means GagWretch.

Which means no.

Which makes me feel better.

Except that my supposed best friend is in love with someone and she doesn't trust me enough to tell me who it is.

But after another week with no clues, I'm starting to think maybe I overreacted. That I heard wrong or . . . I don't know, imagined the whole thing. Or that Erica did. Probably all that happened at the Halloween party was that Sari said hi to some guy, and Erica blew the whole thing out of proportion. Because she's jealous and always has to have something nasty to say about somebody.

And that's all there is to it.

I feel seriously guilty. I can't believe I believed anything Erica Trager would say—particularly about my best friend.

Resolved: Find some way to make it up to Sari that I believed Erica and not her.

On Friday, Sari and I are getting our stuff out of our lockers. I'm about to ask her if she wants to go for cheesecake, my treat, which I figure will be my secret apology.

Then all of a sudden, Sari whispers, "Whatever you do, do not turn around. Okay? And *don't say anything.*"

I freeze. I am staring into my locker. Whatever is happening, I can't see it because the door is blocking my view. I am wondering why Sari doesn't want me to say anything when I hear her say, "Hey, David."

David? Who is David?

Then I hear: "Hey, Ms. Skeleton."

David *Cole*? Sari is talking to David Cole? David Cole is talking to Sari?

"So, how's it going?"

"Good, cool."

I am dying to turn around. But I don't dare.

I hear Sari say, "Doesn't Ms. Brenner bite?"

"Oh, man, she's a dog."

There is more discussion of Ms. Brenner's similarity to a dog. (Looks, nasty personality, fleas.) I don't think this is very fair to Ms. Brenner—or to dogs—but I know that if I say a word, Sari will rip me into tiny pieces and feed me to Ms. Brenner.

Finally, Sari says, "Well, I guess I'll see you around."

And David says, "Yeah, you might."

And then he's gone.

For a few seconds, I stare into my locker, trying to figure out what just happened here.

Finally, I turn around and say, "Sari?"

She's staring down the hall, even though David is long gone. When I say her name again, she hisses, "Shh."

"Sari? What is going on?"

"I don't want to talk about it." Without me, she starts walking, running down the stairs like she's late for something. Except school's over and there's nothing to be late for.

I race after her, follow her out of the building.

For two blocks, Sari walks straight ahead, pretending like she doesn't even know I'm there. I fall in step next to her, pretending like nothing weird is going on. Then, when we are far enough away from Eldridge for it to be safe, I say, "Don't tell me you like David Cole."

"I don't."

"You can't like David Cole."

"I don't 'like' David Cole."

"Yes, you do. And you can't because he's with Thea Melendez."

"I don't 'like' David Cole," says Sari stubbornly. "I am madly, psychotically in love with David Cole."

I stop. Don't even think about it, just . . . stop dead. And stare.

I do not have a clue what to say.

When your best friend tells you she is madly, psychotically in love with one half of the longest-running official couple in the school, what can you say? Do you point out that David is a senior and Thea is a senior and that Sari is seriously outranked? Do you remind her of the time David presented a dozen roses to Thea in the middle of class? Do you recall how Thea sang "The First Time Ever I Saw Your Face" *directly* to David at the Winter Wonder show?

People don't even laugh at David and Thea when they do these things. People think it's nice, romantic. *That's* how much of a couple they are.

David and Thea are gods. Acknowledgment of beings as low as we is strictly forbidden.

Finally I say, "I don't get it."

Sari sighs, flops her arm in the air. "Get *what*?"

"The point of being in love with David Cole. I don't get it."

"Love doesn't have a point," says Sari. "It just *is*."

"But David is madly, psychotically in love with Thea."

"That's what you know," snaps Sari.

Why is that what I know but not what Sari knows? That's what I want to know.

I ask her, and she says, "I'm not just going to blurt out the details of my personal life to you."

Okay, now I want to scream. I want to say, *Why not? Why is now so different from all those* other *times you made me listen to every single detail of your oh-so-precious personal life? Why is suddenly talking to me the worst, stupidest thing you could do?*

But in the end, all I say is, "Well, gee, then I guess I'll just have to go slit my wrists, I'm so disappointed."

"Oh, please." Sari sighs.

Sari is my best friend in the whole world. She is the greatest person in the world. But sometimes it's a problem: Sari thinking that she has a life and that I don't.

Only because we have been friends forever, we keep walking.

A few blocks later, Sari says, "I'm sorry."

I shrug. "It's okay." Meaning: *I could not care less. Hence you have not hurt me. Hence I don't care if you apologize or not.*

"No, it's just . . . I've never felt like this before, and I'm really freaked out."

I glance over at her; she looks upset. I nod, a sign she can go on.

"It's intense," she whispers.

"Uh-huh."

"I don't know what to do."

I'm about to say, *There isn't anything to do. David's with Thea*, but I stop myself in time.

That's the reality.

But I don't think Sari wants to hear that right now.

5

> "Talk." Listening to the chatter, Rana
> raged inside. All these creatures ever
> did was talk. As if talk were action, as
> if talk were food. As if simply by talking
> about it, you could make it so.
>
> —*Hollow Planet: Desert of Souls*

Here's another thing I want to know: Who thought up
the idea of having midterm exams around the holidays?
It totally sucks. How can you get into the Christmas
spirit with doom and disaster hanging over your head?

There are only twenty-three days until Christmas.
Only twelve days until my first midterm.

I have not bought a single present. I have not studied
for a single second.

Here's what I have done: listen to Sari talk about
David.

If you think it's easy being the best friend of a

woman who's madly, psychotically in love, think again.

Every day, I get a David update. Did Sari see David or did she not see David? If she did see David, where did she see him? Did they speak, did they not speak? If they did not speak, was it because he was with Thea? And if they did speak, then it's a five-hour session in which every word, every syllable, is dissected for some hidden meaning that says, *Sari, I love you passionately. Be mine.*

Sometimes I wish we were back to when Sari wouldn't tell me a thing about it.

I don't know about Sari, but I'm not sure that I can survive this obsession. I am in danger of going deaf. My neck is tired from nodding. My vocabulary has shrunk to "Uh-huh" and "I can totally see that."

Like, right now, my arm is in serious danger of withering and falling off. Why? Because Sari is gripping it like she's hanging off a cliff and her life depends on it.

David Cole has just come into the lunchroom. Sari's following him with her eyes, like she can force him to look at her through sheer willpower.

She whispers, "Here, look over here. . . ."

But David doesn't look over here. Instead he goes over to "his" table, the big one in the corner where the soccer crowd hangs.

And sits down right next to Thea.

Sari drops her eyes, tries to pretend she wasn't watching. So she misses David giving Thea a huge kiss on the neck.

To me, David and Thea still look like they're the official couple of Eldridge Alternative. Of course, as Sari said, that's all I know.

She still hasn't told me the reason she knows any different.

And what I'm worried about is that there isn't any reason. That Sari's got an enormous crush on a guy who barely knows she's alive.

David's a senior. He goes out with Thea Melendez. Why would he want to date Sari?

Sari and I are supposed to be studying for exams right now. But forget it now that David is here. Sari's got her math book open, but she keeps looking up to see if David's looking at her.

Guess what? He's not.

Well, I've lost Sari as a study partner, so I might as well get started. I get out my notebook. Just then, Erica Trager and her little crew invade the table next to ours. Erica, of course, is talking nonstop in this obnoxious voice, like everyone in the lunchroom just has to hear what she has to say.

"The units are going to be away." ("The units" is Erica's oh-so-cute term for her parents.) "So it's going to be the most amazing New Year's party ever. I'm having everybody come. . . ."

I could not care less about Erica's amazing New Year's party. So I put my hands over my ears and stare down at my notebook. Out of the corner of my eye, I notice Sari still looking over at David. It's been three days since the last David sighting, a week and a half since he said "Hey" to her in the stairwell.

And that was after we spent twenty minutes waiting for him to pass by so Sari could "accidentally" bump into him.

She looks so sad, I can't stand it.

I put down my pen. "You know what? I need to do some serious present buying."

This gets her attention. Sari loves shopping. She says, "Me too, totally."

"Want to go this weekend?"

Sari nods. "Absolutely. Only, when I get your present, you'll disappear, right?"

I grin. "Same for you."

Then she asks, "Do you think I should get something for him?"

"Who?"

"*Him.*" Sari's annoyed. Like with a billion Hims in the world, I should just know who she's talking about.

The sick thing is, I do.

I shake my head. "No."

"How come?"

I don't know what to say. I mean, if Sari doesn't know why she shouldn't go around buying presents for other people's boyfriends, I don't want to be the one to break the bad news.

Instead, I say, "Well, what would you get him?"

Sari frowns over at the other table, where Thea is getting up. "I don't know. It has to be something cool, but something he cannot show Her."

That's another thing that's happened since Sari fell madly, psychotically in love with David: Thea is no longer Thea. She is now the evil Her.

I ask Sari if 10:00 is too early to start shopping. She says that's good.

So we leave it at that.

Actually, I'm hoping not to buy Sari's present. What I would really like is to give her that portrait of her I started on the last Saturday before school.

One small problem: I have done no work on it whatsoever.

That afternoon, in art class, I get out her picture and stare at it. I don't see how I'm going to be able to give it to her in a few weeks. It's a squiggle, that's all it is. I don't even see what I was thinking when I made it.

I hate it when something I do is no good.

I'm trying to decide if I should rip it up and start all over again when Stella Rothstein stops by my stool and looks over my shoulder.

All she says is, "Hmm."

Which, of course, is code for: *This sucks.*

I haven't decided yet what I think about Stella Rothstein. She has her pluses and minuses. A definite minus is that she wears these long, floaty skirts that are just too *Look, I'm an ARTIST* for words. But so far, she doesn't act like that. She doesn't gush like some art teachers I've had; in fact, she doesn't talk a whole lot. Like the first time she had us work on the vanishing point, I drew this corridor and filled it with blood-soaked demons. She gave that one a *"Well"* with a nod. Which, I think, meant she liked it.

Now she's frowning down at my picture of Sari like she's trying to figure it out.

"It's a portrait," I say, helping her. "The beginning of one."

"Okay." She nods once, doesn't take her eyes off the picture.

I fight the impulse to put my arm over the drawing.

I expected Ms. Rothstein to sort of laugh, say, *Okay, this is a . . . nose? A leg, what?* But she's taking it seriously, and for some reason, that's freaking me out.

Finally I tell her, "I don't think it's very good."

"All right. How come?"

Because it's obviously *not,* I want to say. Instead, I say, "It doesn't look like anything."

"What do you think it should look like?"

"Like the person."

Ms. Rothstein sticks her tongue in her cheek, rocks her head from side to side. "So, what does the person look like?"

"Well, she's got a face, for one thing."

"Yeah, okay. What does she look like?"

I stare at the picture for a long moment. "I can't totally remember."

Ms. Rothstein is about to say something when Carey Phillips calls out a question from the other side of the room. Saying she'll be back, she goes off to help him.

She doesn't come back. And I don't do anything else with Sari's portrait, except decide I'm going to have to get her a present after all.

But at the end of class, when everyone else is gone, she says, "Know what I'd do with that one?"

No one has ever told me what to do with my drawings before. "What?"

"I'd put it aside. Let it sit."

I nod. Ms. Rothstein starts gathering up pens and brushes and putting them back in their jars.

She says, "You know, I'm teaching a class next semester on portraiture. You should sign up for it."

I nod. I am definitely going to try and get into that class.

The night before our big shopping expedition, I make out my list. It's pretty short this year, which is good because I have *no* money.

Here's my list:

DAD—Big new book on Vietnam.
MOM—New Tracy Chapman CD.
NOBO—Pup Pops in assorted flavors.
SARI—"Women Who Love Men Who Don't Love Them"

I don't think I'll really have the guts to get Sari that book. But I like to think I will.

At 9:30 in the morning, as I take the bus to meet Sari downtown, I am totally psyched.

By 11:00 I am totally frustrated.

Sari mopes all through the first store while I buy my dad's book. Then she sighs and droops all around Pet Palace. She won't even help me decide if I should get Nobo a grape-flavored Pup Pop or a peanut-butter flavored one.

When we leave Pet Palace, I say, "Okay, where to?"

Sari shrugs.

Clearly, I have no choice. If I want Sari to behave like a living, sentient being, there's only one thing to do.

So I do it. "You want to look for something for Lord God Cole?"

Sari's eyes light up. "Can we?"

I nod. Deranged with excitement, Sari drags me off to one of those trendoid gadget places. You know the ones, where they have voice-operated electric can openers for a thousand bucks.

Nothing in this place costs less than fifty dollars. As we wander past the glass cases, I think she can't really be thinking of spending all that money on David Cole. He'll laugh in her face.

Unless, unless . . . she knows he won't. But how can she know that?

Because I want to find out just how crazy she is, I point to a watch that costs five hundred dollars and say, "That's cool."

Sari wrinkles her nose. "Yeah, but he'd have to hide it from *Her.*"

As we wander over to the stereo department, I say, "Sar? Can I ask you something?"

"Sure."

"Did you and David . . . ?" Argh, how do I put this? "Did something happen at the Halloween dance?"

Sari doesn't say anything. She just stares at the stereos. Meanwhile, my mind is reeling with possibilities. What can I say? I have this very lurid imagination.

"Sari?"

"No. I mean—" She stops, like she's trying to decide what really did happen. "Nothing *happened* happened. But something happened."

I nod like this makes total sense.

"I mean, all we did was talk."

I nod again, feeling like some creepy talk-show host.

I half expect to see under Sari's head: SHE'S IN LOVE WITH ANOTHER WOMAN'S MAN.

"But . . . I don't know. I don't know how to explain it. He was talking about how people have these expectations of you, these preconceived notions of who you are, and how that can be really limiting."

"And he was talking about Thea."

"Well, yeah, I thought so. She wants them to get engaged before they go to college. How sad can you be?"

"And did he say he liked you?"

Sari gives me this look. "It was kind of obvious."

In the end, we don't find anything for David Cole. Everything's either not cool enough or so cool that Thea would notice it. By this time, I am so exhausted, I keep checking my pulse to see if I still have one. On the bus, I hold my shopping bags in my lap and wonder if I can fall asleep on them.

We are halfway home when Sari asks, "Are you going to Erica Trager's New Year's party?"

Now it's my turn to give her a look. "Yeah, right after I gouge my eyes out with a fork. Are you kidding?"

I hate Erica Trager. Which means I don't spend a lot of time in her company. Which means there are a million things I'd rather do—like tiptoe across nails—than go to her party.

All of which Sari knows. So why is she asking me if I'm going to Erica Trager's party?

"Because I'm going," she says. "And I want you to come with me."

"Why?"

"Because . . . ," she starts, then sighs. "Look, never mind why—just come. Please?"

She's staring at me, waiting for my answer.

I say, "David Cole will be at this party."

Sari says, "Ye-ah," in that voice I hate, the voice that says, *I know all about the world and you don't.*

"That's why you want to go."

Sari nods.

"I have to see him alone," she says urgently. "Away from school . . . away from *Her.*"

"But won't Thea be there?"

"She's going to be in Florida to see her grandparents. Please come, please." Sari's grabbing my arm. For a weird moment, it feels like she's going to cry. "I can't let this not happen. This is so important to me."

I want to tell her she doesn't need me, that I'm totally irrelevant here, that probably seeing her with me will be enough to put David Cole off for life.

But I know what she means. You need your friends when you're doing the riskiest thing you've ever done.

Besides, after the Halloween disaster, I did sort of promise Sari I might go to a party with her.

I say, "I have to ask my parents."

Sari shrieks with happiness. "No, you don't. Just tell them you're staying over at my house."

I can't do that. I don't know why not, I just can't. It's not that I'm so afraid of getting caught. It's just that I don't like to lie to my parents. I have a few times, and it always feels like there's something bad between us, like we're living in different worlds.

Besides, part of me is really hoping they'll say I can't go.

For the record, Sari never did ask me to disappear so she could buy me a present.

No big deal, I guess.

At dinner that night, I say, "Is it okay if I go to a New Year's party at Erica Trager's house?"

My mom says, "Who's Erica Trager?"

"A jerk."

My dad asks, "If she's a jerk, why're you going to her party?"

"Sari wants me to." I push my mashed potatoes into a little mountain. "She's all hooked on some guy." I add this because I think it makes me sound less pathetic, making Sari sound more pathetic.

My dad asks, "Why isn't she going with the guy?"

"Because the guy is quite 'cool' and dating someone else." My parents look at each other. "She's got some stupid crush on him."

My mom says, "Do you want to go?"

I poke at the mashed-potato mountain. "Not really. But Sari wants me to."

There's a little silence. Then my mom says, "Then, okay . . . I guess."

She smiles at me, wanting me to be happy she said yes.

Instead, I stick my fork in the middle of the mashed potatoes to see if it will stay standing up.

After dinner, I call Sari. "I can go."

"Great." She sounds hugely relieved.

"Yeah, I just have to be home, like, right after midnight."

"Cool." She says this like it doesn't matter, and for a second, I wonder why. Cool because she has to be home at midnight too? Or cool because, by then, she'll be passionately entwined with David Cole and won't care if I am there or not?

Looking at my desk, I realize it's time for me to stop thinking about Sari and David Cole. If I don't start studying soon, I'm going to be in serious trouble.

Except . . .

Except first, I think I have to get a soda.

When I go to the kitchen, my dad's there, washing the dishes.

He puts a glass on the drying rack and says, "How's the studying going?"

"It's . . . about to be going really well." I get a soda out of the fridge.

"Glad to hear it."

My dad turns off the faucet and wipes his hands. "So, this New Year's thing."

"Yeah?"

"You're going 'cause Sari's going?"

"Well, she wants me there." I climb up on the counter and let my legs swing.

"In case this 'cool guy' doesn't come through?"

I smile. "Yeah."

"So how cool is this guy?"

"So cool he doesn't know she's alive."

My dad throws his head back and laughs. I smile along with him. I love making my dad laugh.

Then he shakes his head. "I don't know. If Sari's got a crush on him, I'd say chances are he knows she's alive."

"What do you mean?"

"Well, hon . . ." My dad shrugs in this way I can tell means he wishes I hadn't asked. "She's a pretty girl. Guys tend to notice interest from someone like that."

All the happiness drains right out of me. I don't know why. It's not like my dad has told me any big secret. Sari is pretty, I know that. And guys do notice her. But somehow, my dad telling me that is like saying he's noticed it too, and that makes me feel very weird.

For a split second, I want to ask him if he thinks I'm pretty. And then I totally don't.

I slide off the counter and take my soda. "I think I need to do the study thing," I say, and go back down the hall to my room.

6

Rana advanced with stealth. It was essential to attract no attention, for she was deep within enemy territory, and recognition meant death.

—*Hollow Planet: Thorvald's Hammer*

I finished my last exam five minutes ago. I am sitting in the middle stall of the bathroom.

My brain has ceased to function. I am too tired even to go home.

Don't ask me how I did, because I have no idea. I've slept two minutes in the last week. My hand still feels like it's holding a pen, and I can't get the verb *tenir* in the subjunctive out of my head.

I guess I should leave. I don't think the school is going to let me go into a coma here.

Which is basically all I want to do.

It's Saturday. I have slept twenty-three out of the last twenty-four hours, and now feel almost normal again.

I hear my mom knocking on the door. "Jess? It's Sari on the phone for you."

Between the last day of classes and New Year's Eve, Sari calls me every single day to talk about the party.

"What time do you think we should get there?"

"How 'bout never?"

"Ha-ha. I think we should get there at, like, nine thirty."

"Sure. Then we can leave at, like, nine thirty-five."

Sari pretends not to hear this. "I cannot decide what to wear."

"You'll look great, whatever you wear."

"Yeah, right." Sari sighs. "Hey, can you do me the biggest favor?"

"What?"

"When you come over before the party, bring the Book?"

"Sure."

"I want to ask it right before the party—you know, when the energy is strong." Sari tries to say it like she's joking, but I can tell she's deadly serious.

"Sure, whatever."

"Thanks, I owe you. Whatever favor, just ask."

Unfortunately, the only favor I want is not to go to this party. I know it's pathetic, but I'm actually a little nervous. Some of these parties have gotten pretty wild. One girl passed out once, and they had to take her to the emergency room. Another time, some guy stole something of Erica's dad's, and there was this whole big thing before it was returned.

A few days later, my mother tries to lay down some rules. "Be home by twelve."

I think: *Twelve? Try ten thirty.* No way can I stay in close proximity to Erica Trager for three whole hours.

"And call if things get too much."

Now she's being bizarre. "Ma."

"If things get out of hand, and you want us to come get you, just call."

I can't imagine what my mom thinks is going to happen. Like someone's going to drop acid in my Pepsi and sell me into slavery. More likely, I'll just puke out of boredom.

I say this to her, and she says, "I know. It's just your first high school party, and I want you to know we have you covered if you need it."

"Okay, Ma."

She pretends she's moving some hair out of my eyes, but I can tell it's just an excuse to touch me.

Yes! I have scored three B+'s, one B-, and an A-. Life is amazing and perfect.

At least, it would be if I didn't have to go to this stupid party.

On the big day, I look through my closet and all my drawers and realize one thing: I have no social life.

Because, theoretically, if I did have a social life, I might have some clothes to go with it.

It's two hours before I have to be at Sari's, and all I have is the stuff I wear to school, five thousand T-shirts, and two revolting skirts my mom makes me wear when we go somewhere fancy.

I wonder if I can call Sari and tell her I have come down with plague.

Finally, I throw on some jeans, my most obnoxious T-shirt, run out the door, and head over to Sari's. Really, it doesn't matter what I wear. In case you haven't figured it out yet, I am not one of those people everyone looks at to spot the latest trends. *Ooh, what's Jess Horvath wearing? Quick, go out and buy one just like it . . . and burn it.*

"Did you bring the Book?" This is the first thing Sari demands when she opens the door.

I pull it out of my coat pocket, hold it up.

"Cool." She lets me in, closes the door. "Let me see what you're wearing."

I open my coat, show her.

She checks it out. "I think you should borrow something of mine."

"Get real." I pull the coat closed.

Now that Sari's done staring at me, it's my turn to stare at her. I've never seen her so dressed up. At least, not like this. Everything is short and tight, and, well, there isn't much of it. I guess to someone like David Cole, it'll look great, but it looks weird to me. I want to put a coat over her.

"Let's go to my room," she says, pulling me past the living room before I even have a chance to say hi to her parents. They're watching TV. I wave, but they don't see me.

In her room, Sari shuts the door and starts shoving stuff out of the way so we can sit down in the middle of the floor, the way we do at my house. Her room has basically exploded. Every drawer is open, clothes are sprawled everywhere: over her chair, on her bed, hanging over her closet door. I didn't think it was possible for anyone to have this many clothes.

Finally Sari kicks the last of the mess aside and sits down. Waving her hands in the air, she says, "Okay, come on, let's go."

Lifting the Book, I say, "Will you speak the words?"

Sari shuts her eyes tight. Her hands are fists as she says, "Tell us, O Book, how does the future look?"

I wait. When Sari doesn't say anything, I say, "Ready?"

Sari nods. I hand her the Book. Taking a deep breath, she opens it and points.

For a second, she looks away.

Then she holds the Book out. "You read it."

I want to say, *No, I don't want the responsibility.* Sari's so flipped with nerves, I feel like she'll go nuclear if the Book doesn't tell her what she wants to hear. But I pull the Book closer and read, "'I am doubtful whether I was at heart sorry or glad when—'"

I stop. The rules are that you read to the end of the line.

Sari frowns. "When what?"

"Well, after that, it's 'when my school days drew to an end, and the time came for my leaving Doctor Strong's.'"

Sari rolls her eyes. "Oh, great. What does that mean?"

"Well, it's sort of about growing up." I shrug. "Leaving things behind maybe."

Agitated, Sari shakes her head. "Whatever. I don't get it." She scrambles up, grabs her coat. "We gotta go, we're going to be late."

I slide the Book back into my pocket and follow Sari. As we go by the living room, she rushes by without saying anything. I call, "Good night, Mr. and Mrs. Aaronsohn."

Then, as Sari closes the door, I hear her mother call, "'Night, girls."

Erica's building is one of those places where the second you walk into the lobby, you know that seriously rich people live there. The doorman is wearing an overcoat and gives us a suspicious look as we come in. Immediately, I have the impulse to hawk up a gob of spit and leave it on one of the enormous mirrors or smear it on the oak paneling.

Sari doesn't seem to notice. Striding to the elevator, she presses the button, one, two, three times. Then she shoves her hands in her pockets and watches the floor lights as the elevator comes down.

She says to me, "Okay, whatever you do, do not leave me alone."

"Yeah, right. Like I'm going to go party down in the VIP room."

"I'm serious."

The elevator reaches the lobby. We stand aside as two people, all dressed up, get out.

In the elevator, I say, "What do you want me to do when you see . . . *Him?*"

Sari shakes her head. "I bet he doesn't even come. And you know what, even if he does? He's gonna totally ignore me."

"He won't ignore you, Sari." I say this because I am Sari's friend, not because I necessarily know this to be true.

So I tell her, "You know what I bet? I bet so many guys are hanging around you, David Cole can't even get near you."

Sari rolls her eyes. "Oh, *great.*"

We get out of the elevator and start walking down the hall to Erica's apartment. I start feeling nervous again.

If you hate it, I tell myself for the hundredth time, *you can leave.*

Five seconds after we walk in the door, I want to say to Sari, *Okay, let's leave.*

Right away, the whole thing feels wrong.

For one thing, the music is loud. I mean, really loud. Nobody can hear anybody unless they yell right in your ear. And a lot of the lights are turned off, so you can't see who's here unless you fall over them. And there are a million people here. There's a lot of screaming. A lot of laughing. Two guys are racing from room to room spraying Silly String on people. Some other people have torn all the cushions off the couch and are whaling away at each other. I feel like I don't know any of them, even if I've been going to school with them for forever. Everyone just feels . . . different.

I look over at Sari, hoping she feels like I do, that she wants to get out of here.

She says, "Let's go get something to drink."

So we go to the kitchen, and there's Coke and Sprite. And Budweiser. And Heineken. And even a bottle of real liquor.

I stare at the beer. I stare even more when Sari pops a can and hands it to me.

"No."

"Come on." She gives me a look like, *Don't be dumb.*

"Sari, I totally mean it. No."

For some reason, I feel like I might start screaming.

"'Kay." Sari starts drinking it herself. I try to think of something sarcastic to say that might stop her. But I can't.

While I'm thinking, this girl Christie Siegler comes up to Sari and says, "Hey." And Sari shrieks, "Hey!" and they hug like they're best friends, even though I can't remember Sari ever mentioning Christie before.

But Christie dates Nicky Williams, one of David's best friends. Hence the sudden wonderfulness of Christie.

While they talk, I look around the kitchen to see if there's anyone else here I can talk to. I mean, it's not like Sari's the only one who can talk to other human beings.

Unfortunately it doesn't look like a lot of human beings are at this party.

Only a lot of raving maniacs.

I pour myself a Sprite, try not to look like I'm just waiting around for Sari to remember I exist. For a few seconds, I even try to stand next to this other group, like I'm with them. But then one of them gives me this look that says, *Get away from us or die.*

So I get away from them.

And that's when I realize that Sari has split.

After all that "Don't leave me alone" stuff . . . she's gone.

For a second, I think, *Great, now I can leave.*

But then I think, *If I leave, I will be a total loser. Leave, and I might as well forget ever having a social life in high school.*

Taking my Sprite, I leave the kitchen and walk slowly back into the living room. These guys are mostly sophomores, and I don't know any of them well enough to talk to. Besides, they all seem . . . well, drunk. A few of them have even laid a broom on the floor and are taking turns walking on it to see if they can walk in a straight line. Every time one falls off, they all cackle hysterically. As Rachael Bennett steps on the broom, I feel the urge to push her off, watch her fall over.

For a little while, I stand by this bookcase and check out what Erica's parents read. From the look of it, they are only marginally more intelligent than Erica. My father would laugh at these books. He would say that people who have books like this in their house deserve to be shot.

No one is talking to me. I try to look like I prefer it that way.

I duck as Michael Potok sprays Leisel Franklin with a can of Bud. In that second, I hate Michael Potok. I want to hit him. I want to take the can of beer and smash it in his face.

I wander down the hall, which is packed with idiot laughing people. I find a little spot on the floor and sit down. For a while, I just watch everything that's going on. I feel like some invisible being, like an alien or a spirit no one can see. It's not a bad thing to be. People do very interesting things when they don't know anyone's watching.

I see two guys shooting condoms at each other like they're rubber bands.

I hear a girl say something really cruel about another girl who's supposedly her best friend.

I see two people come out of the bathroom. A guy and a girl. They've been in there forever. The guy's a senior, the girl's a sophomore. She looks upset to me. The guy keeps walking down the hall, but she stops and slides down to the floor right near me.

I ask, "Are you okay?"

She gives me a nasty look, says, "Yeah."

I have made a mistake. I have spoken. My cover's blown, and I decide to move on.

There are beer cans everywhere. I kick one, and it spills all over the floor.

Good.

I don't know why I'm so angry. But it feels good to be angry. It feels good to hate these people, to not feel like one of them.

My mom was all worried I couldn't handle something like this. I can handle it just fine.

Then I see David Cole come down the hall. Thea's not with him.

I wonder where Sari is. If she knows David is here. I think about trying to find her and tell her. But I decide no. Let her find out for herself.

I decide to keep moving. I find Erica's parents' room. The door is closed and has a big sign on it: MY PARENTS' ROOM. STAY OUT. So Erica isn't totally stupid.

Out of curiosity, I open the door. It's dark, but I can see two other people who didn't pay attention to the sign.

I shut the door and head back toward the living room. On the way, I run into Danny. Literally.

"Hi," says Danny. Really loud. Like meeting me is the greatest thing that ever happened to him.

"Danny," I ask, "what's that in your hand?"

He offers the bottle. "You want a sip?"

"No."

Danny isn't just drunk. He's really drunk. Like he can hardly stand up, he's so trashed. I can't believe these people let Danny get drunk. He's just a kid. I mean, yeah, he's my age, but he's a numbnut. I'll bet a million dollars he never drank before in his life.

"Danny, did you come here with someone?"

He looks around. "Philip, but I don't know where he is."

Philip. One of the jerkiest guys in our class. It figures.

"How are you getting home?"

He grins. "I'm not ready to leave." He swigs the rest of the beer. Only he kind of stumbles because he moves his arm too fast and falls against the wall.

"Danny, are you okay?"

"I don't know."

"Do you feel sick?" I'm getting scared now. People can die from drinking too much. Only I don't know what to do, and believe me, no one around is going to help me. They're too busy yelling and singing and drinking.

Danny says, "I think I have to throw up."

Oh, God, one of my least-favorite things in the world. I pound on the bathroom door. Someone yells back, "Wait a minute." I do wait a minute, but nothing happens. There's probably another bathroom somewhere, but I don't know where it is, so I drag Danny into the kitchen. Yelling, "Out of the way, out of the way," I push him up against the sink.

Where he immediately hurls.

Someone screams, "Oh, gross." Everyone backs off, saying things like, "Give me a break." "God, get him out of here." "What a geek."

A few people look at Danny like they might want to help, but they walk out like everybody else.

Someone has to get Danny home. I tell Danny to stay where he is, and I go to find Sari to tell her I'm leaving. After looking everywhere, I finally find her in Erica's room. She's sitting on the bed, yakking with a bunch of people: Kara Davis and Andy Richman and John Howard and . . . David Cole.

David's sitting sort of next to her. But she's on the bed, and he's on the floor. So he's sitting by her leg.

Right by her leg. Like, they're touching.

If I were Thea, I would not like this scene at all.

I say, "Sari?" She doesn't hear me right away, so I have to say again, "Sari?"

She looks up. "Oh, hey, where'd you go?"

Yeah, like you, Miss Don't Leave Me, didn't disappear. I

would like very much to say this, but Danny's probably puking on a priceless rug somewhere.

I tell her, "I'm leaving."

"Why?"

"I have to take Danny home."

This gets a big laugh. Particularly from Lord God David Cole.

"Danny?" Sari makes a face, playing it up for David. "He's sick."

Kara says, "The geek who puked in the sink," and Sari says, "Eeuuw."

I don't like Sari right now. I don't like her at all. If this is who she's going to be, I don't want to know her.

"Well, anyway," I say, "I'm leaving."

For a second, Sari looks unsure. "Come back after."

Yeah, I think, *in case David Cole dumps you. Screw you, Sari.*

I go back to the kitchen, but Danny isn't there anymore. I ask a few people, but no one knows where he's gone.

So I think, *Screw Danny,* and leave.

A half hour later, I'm home. It's only 11:30. My parents are in the living room.

"How was it?" my mom calls when I pass by.

"Okay." I stop but don't sit down.

My dad asks, "Did Sari's dream man show up?"

"Yeah, he showed up."

I can tell they want all the details. But I just want to say good night and go to bed.

So that's what I do.

The next morning, while I'm eating breakfast, I make my very first New Year's resolutions:

1. I am never going to drink. Ever.
2. I am never speaking to Sari again.

I've crossed Danny off my list too. (Assuming he survived.) Which means I could end up spending the rest of my high school years totally alone.

That's okay. Frankly, this morning, I'm not that hot on the human race.

After breakfast, I take Nobo for a long walk and let him play with a poodle named Lola. I think Nobo's in love, but it's never going to work out. Lola is way more glamorous than he is.

As we walk home, I tell him that love is very overrated. Particularly with beautiful, glamorous types like Lola.

That afternoon, I'm farting around on the Web when the phone rings. We have two phones, one in my room, one in the kitchen. You know how sometimes you just know who's calling? And you sort of want to speak to them, and you also sort of don't, so you leave the whole thing up to fate?

That's what I do. I decide that if my mom or dad gets to the phone and it's Sari, I'll take the call. But if they don't pick it up and she leaves a message on the machine, I won't call back.

All of a sudden, the phone stops ringing. Either my parents or the machine has answered.

Then I hear my mom call, "Jess? Sari."

I go to the phone and pick up. I say, "Okay, Ma," into it, and wait for her to hang up. When she does, I say, "Hi."

So much for New Year's resolutions.

There's a long silence at the other end. So, Sari feels a little weird calling. Good, she should feel weird. She should, in my opinion, be figuring out how to beg my forgiveness for abandoning me at that jerk-off party.

Finally, Sari says, "Hey, how are you?"

"I'm okay. How are you?"

"Good, I'm great."

That's not what I want to hear. Something more along the lines of, *I'm miserable and feel like puking*— that's what I want to hear.

Except Sari doesn't sound *that* great, if you know what I mean. She sounds like she knows I want her to be miserable and she's saying, *Screw you, I'm not.* And even though I'm still pissed at her, I have to admit, a good friend doesn't go around hoping you're miserable because you got to hang with the man of your dreams.

I ask her, "How late did you stay?"

"Oh, God, like, till three, three thirty."

In other words: *I didn't miss you a bit, you loser.*

Then she says, "You missed some funny stuff."

"Oh, yeah?"

"Chloe Friedlander stuck Erica's mom's fur coat in the toilet."

This, I can totally believe. Chloe is an animal rights freak. Won't dissect anything, starts crying in any movie with an animal in it, wears a big anti-fur button. I am not that into animal rights, but my respect for Chloe has suddenly gone up.

"How'd she get the whole coat in?"

"Well, not the whole thing, just the sleeve. But then she flushed it, to make it go down? And the toilet flooded. Water *everywhere*." Sari laughs.

"Did Erica freak?"

"Completely."

"I wish I'd seen that."

After a moment, Sari says, "Yeah, why'd you leave?"

There are a lot of different answers to this question, and I'm not sure which one I want to give. Finally, I say, "I don't know, the whole thing just got kind of intense for me."

Which is, as they say, the truth, but not the whole truth, and nothing but the truth. Call me a big fat wimp. I don't feel like yelling at her.

And when Sari says, "Yeah, things did kind of get out of hand," I feel like we're friends again.

Since we're friends, I have to ask her the thing I know she's dying to tell me about. "So, what happened with David?"

"Uh, stuff happened."

"Yeah?"

"Yeah, stuff definitely happened."

Then Sari tells me what happened. What they did. Or rather, what she did.

I can't believe my friend has done this. I don't know everything Sari's done, she doesn't always tell me. But I know she's never done this before. There are bases, aren't there? Steps you take. You work your way up to this kind of thing. You don't just do it to some boy in a bathroom with a hundred people standing on the other side of the door.

Even if the boy is David Cole. Even if you are madly, psychotically in love.

"He said I was really good at it," Sari tells me. Then she tells me something I don't want to know, a detail that proves, yes, she has really done this. That soon she will be having sex, and I will have to worry about her getting pregnant. I make a promise: I will not let Sari go to the clinic by herself. I will even lend her money if I have to.

I ask, "How do you feel?"

"Fine." She sounds like it's weird that I asked. "It's no big deal."

"So, are you guys going out now?"

"I don't know. We didn't really talk about it."

Sari is still sounding very cool about it, but I can tell: She wanted to talk about it.

"He said he would call me."

"Well . . . wow," I say. Because I'm out of things to say.

"Yeah," says Sari. Who, it seems, is also out of things to say.

7

It was a time of judgment. Some would
be found worthy. Others would not.

—*Hollow Planet: The Darkening Storm*

After I hang up the phone, I go and sit on my bed. I
wrap my arms around my legs and fold up as tight as I
can. I lean my chin on my knees, dig in hard, until I am
one smooth, solid piece of stone.

I close my eyes, try to imagine being a rock. It would
not be the worst thing. It happens to Thor in the second *Hollow Planet* book. He's turned into a boulder,
right near the ocean. He ends up making the sea an ally,
and that's how Rana and her army win . . . some battle,
I don't exactly remember.

I have this weird feeling that I just had my last
conversation ever with Sari.

Which is stupid. I'm going to see her in school on Monday.

But I can't help it. I keep feeling that something is over. That it's just . . . gone, and there's nothing I can do to get it back.

For a second I open my eyes and see my Hollow Planet drawings all over the wall. I hate them. They look sad and pathetic and childish. They make my room look like a five-year-old's.

I wrap my arms even tighter around my legs, twist my hands together until the skin feels like it's going to rip, slide right off the bone. I desperately want to destroy all the pictures.

But part of me knows that even if I hate them, they're mine. And I can't destroy them because of that.

I'm still staring at the pictures when my mom knocks on the door and calls me in for dinner. My dad's at the library, so it's just my mom and me tonight. And Nobo, waiting under the table for whatever drops.

I don't really feel like eating, so I just shove my food around the plate. If my mom notices, she doesn't say anything.

Instead she asks if I'm looking forward to going back to school.

I roll my eyes at her. "Okay," she says, "forget school. How's Sari doing?"

"Good. I guess. I don't know."

"Whatever happened with that guy?"

Now, I don't know how to answer that one. I mean, I know what's happened. I just don't know how to put it in "Mom-speak."

"You never really told us how the party went."

"It sucked."

My mom makes a face. She's annoyed I thought the party sucked. My mom would like me to like things like parties. She would like me to be easy and popular. To have a million friends and never hate anyone or get pissed off.

I nudge my green beans to the left side of the plate. "Parties aren't for people like me, Ma."

"What does that mean?" She's smiling at me like, *What a doof of a daughter I have.* But she doesn't know. She doesn't know anything about Eldridge. That's why she thinks you can look forward to going back there.

"Parties are elitist gatherings for popular people."

"And you're not 'popular.'" She's still smiling.

"No, Ma. I hate to break it to you."

"You have friends."

I think: *Do I?*

"'Friends' isn't popular," I tell my mom. "Popular is like . . . really smart, or pretty, or hot. Like Sari. Sari could be popular."

That's as close as I'm going to get to discussing the whole Sari/David Cole thing with my mother.

"Oh," she says. "Because Sari's 'hot.'"

Okay, discussing "hot" with my mother is ten out of ten on a scale of bizarreness.

I shrug. "Kind of."

"You know," she says, "that kind of thing isn't all that important. It doesn't usually last very long."

"It lasts," I say, getting all defensive, like it's in my interest that hot people keep their power. "What are you saying, that older women aren't attractive?" I want to say "sexy," but you know how it is. Around your parents, those words jam up in your throat. *Hey, Ma, I think that's sexy.* . . . GagWretch.

"I'm not saying that at all. I'm just saying the kind of thing you're talking about doesn't last because it's usually about being young and . . . not knowing."

"Actually, I think it's more about . . . knowing. If you know what I mean."

My mom smiles. "You think that because you're young."

Okay, yes, true, but wrong. Because the fact is, I am right and my mother is not. As with all inborn advantages, hotness gives you that essential self-confidence and sense of power that you can rely on forever. Maybe you're not always going to look as amazing as you do now, but hotness isn't even about looks. It's about confidence and . . . knowing. That's the only way I can describe it. And once you got it, you can always flaunt it.

That's how I see it, anyway.

I can tell from the way my mom is looking at me that she doesn't see it that way at all. But like I said, there's a lot she doesn't know about how things are. She likes to think that life is like it is in catalogs: these perfect scenes of happiness, where everything's clean and everyone's thin and smiling.

The problem is, I definitely do not live in that world.

Another problem: I'm not sure what world I do live in.

The next morning, I am on the bus. On my way back to Eldridge.

I remember how, on the first day of high school, Sari and I made this very specific plan to meet. Where, what time, everything.

I guess today we just see each other when we see each other.

I wonder if anyone else knows what happened at Erica's party. I wonder if Thea knows.

Maybe David told her. When she came back from seeing her grandparents, maybe he said, *It's all over between us. I found my true love. She is Sari Aaronsohn. My passion for her shall never die.*

That's definitely what Sari's hoping.

The bus rolls into a tunnel, and I try to think what it will be like if David and Sari become the new Official Eldridge Couple.

Everyone will think they are amazing and cool.

And Sari will never speak to me again.

My Nice Self says that will never happen.

My Rotten Self says it will.

The bus halts, sighs, like all the air is going out of its tires, and sinks so people can get off. I push the back door hard; they always close it on you too fast.

As I walk toward the school, I tell myself I have to be happy for Sari. I have to pretend that this is this great thing, and that she's so lucky, and that David's the most amazing guy in the world.

A lot of people are hanging out on the steps of the school. I look for Sari, but I don't see her.

Then I see something else and stop dead, right where I am.

I think: *It's funny how once you know one little thing*

about a person, you can never see them the same way again.

For example, knowing what David Cole did with Sari in the bathroom at Erica Trager's party . . . well, it just gives me a whole new perspective on the sight of David and Thea making out on the Eldridge steps.

For what seems like minutes, I just stare. I can't believe this. I mean, tongues are going here. Saliva is definitely being exchanged.

If I were the person I would like to be, I would walk straight up to David, pull him off Thea, and say, *Hi, there. Remember me? I'm Sari's friend. Remember Sari?*

But I'm not that person yet, so I just run up the stairs and into the building.

Okay, the absolute last thing that can happen now is that I run into Sari. Even if I don't say a word, I feel like what I just saw is all over my face, like chicken pox.

I can't stop staring. I've been inside for two, three minutes, and my eyes are still wide open.

I blink a few times, to get my eyes to look normal. I have to think this through. In private, somewhere I won't run into Sari. Everyone is headed upstairs, so I go downstairs to the lunchroom. This time in the morning, no one will be there. I sneak inside, go sit at one of the tables in the corner . . . and think and think and think.

I don't get it. I totally don't get it. What are David and Thea doing in a passionate embrace? Why hasn't he told her it's all over between them?

He wasn't kissing her to be nice, either. You could tell he was into it. And it was cold out—but not *that* cold.

How could he do that? After what happened with Sari?

Maybe he's sorry it happened. Maybe he feels horribly guilty for doing that to Thea.

But what about what he's doing to Sari? It's so unfair.

I have to tell her.

She will absolutely freak.

I should practice. Decide what I'm going to say. Taking a deep breath, I start.

Sari . . .

She's going to be really upset. I should make sure we're someplace alone. Not in the hall, where everyone can see.

Okay, stop stalling.

Sari, I saw David and Thea. They were kissing.

Gag. I can't say that. It sounds totally infantile: *Ooh, they were kissing.*

Maybe I should just ask her if she's seen David. Maybe she already knows.

I'll say that I saw them. And then I'll let her ask me how they looked. And then I can say something like, *Well, pretty friendly.*

Sari will say, *Friendly how?*

Then I'll have to say, *They were kissing.*

But she might want specific details. She could say something like, *How were they kissing? Like sad? On the cheek . . . or was Thea kissing him?*

I'll say, *Really kissing. Like, making out.*

And then Sari will say . . .

Sari will say, *How do you know what "really kissing" is?*

Sari will say, *What do you know about making out?*

And I'll shoot back, *Maybe nothing at all. But I know it when I see it.*

Which sounds dumb even to me.

Suddenly, I realize, I'm all pissed off at Sari, and I haven't even seen her yet. I remind myself that she hasn't said any of these things to me, that it's all in my head.

But she could say those things. She could absolutely say them.

Because the fact is, she is not going to want to believe any of this.

So . . . maybe I shouldn't tell her.

I mean, it's true: I don't actually know what's going on. And if I tell her something bad about David that turns out to be wrong, it's very, very possible that Sari would never forgive me.

Okay, here's the plan. I will tell her *only* if she asks me directly, *Have you seen David?*

When I finally find Sari by the lockers, she's not screaming and throwing things, so I know she hasn't seen David and Thea.

As we put our stuff away, she whispers, "Have you seen him?"

I freeze. Here it is. I said I would tell her if she asked—and she asked. I open my mouth, ready to destroy the life of my best friend. . . .

But I can't do it. I just can't. There are all these people around, for one thing. I don't want them to see Sari cry. I don't want to see her cry.

Without really meaning to, I shake my head.

Sari frowns, shuts her locker. "He hasn't called yet."

I say, "He probably hasn't had a chance."

"Yeah." Sari takes a deep breath, rocks on the balls of

her feet. "I'm having total withdrawal symptoms. Like, I have to see him, now."

I'm thinking: *Now is probably a much better time to see David than ten minutes ago.*

People are pushing past us, heading up to the Hall of Happy Thought. In five minutes, there's an assembly on fire safety. "Let's go." I pull Sari by the arm. "Maybe he's waiting upstairs."

All I can say is, if the fire alarm ever does ring, and there is an inferno raging through the building, Sari is going to be in big trouble. She will have absolutely no idea which stairs to use and which exits to look for.

Sari has not listened to a word of the lecture. Since we got here, all she has done is look for David. The whole time, while Crazy Maisie tells us how to save our lives, Sari's been standing on her tiptoes, her head up, straining to see to the edge of the crowd, for any sign of her beloved.

So far, no sign.

Actually, I too am keeping an eye out for David. But unlike Sari, I dread the thought of seeing him. I dread what will happen when Sari sees him with Thea.

Luckily—or unluckily—David never shows. It's not surprising. The truly cool almost always cut out of assemblies. As we file out of the gym, I whisper, "He's probably down at the park wall. Having a smoke."

Which is not a lie. Because he probably is.

Only with Thea.

On the stairs, I see Danny Oriel. He's a few people ahead of me, but as he turns the corner, he looks up and sees me.

He waves.

I look away, pretend not to see him. After Erica Trager's party, there's no way I am ever speaking to Danny Oriel again.

And of course, because everything isn't crazy *enough*, I have a totally new schedule this semester. Now I don't know where I am or what time I'm supposed to be there!

It has been almost three days since the party—Sunday, Monday, and half of today—and David still hasn't called. Not only that, he hasn't said a word to Sari. Not even "Hello," like he used to.

Last night, Sari asked me to call her to make sure her phone was working.

It was.

Then we spent an hour discussing why David hasn't called. Sari thinks he can't call, because it's not safe.

"Thea's probably on his case all the time. I bet she knows something's going on, and she doesn't let him out of her sight."

I waited a second, then said, "Yeah, that's probably it."

Part of me really wanted to tell Sari the truth. But the other part of me, the stronger part, said, *No way.*

After I hung up with her, the parts argued until I went to sleep. So this morning, I woke up and made a rule: No more thinking about David and Sari until something actually happens. The second either of their names comes into my head, hit the DELETE key.

You have a life, I tell myself. *You have other things to think about than David and Sari and Thea.*

Oh, yeah? Like what?

I had to think about that one for a second, but I did come up with something: Ms. Rothstein's portrait class. Today is the first day, and I am determined not to go into her class obsessing about Sari and David.

All day, I work on clearing my mind. By the time I have art, which is my last class of the day, I have only thought about David and Sari three times—a vast improvement. As I walk up the stairs to the art studio, I think: *You are an artist. Don't be distracted by blah-blah like love and romance and jerky guys.*

The art studio is next to the gym. When I get to the fifth floor, there's a class going on, and I nearly get my head taken off by a volleyball.

I wait for a lull in the game so I can cross the gym. I totally don't get sports. All these people running after a ball, shrieking, "I got it, I got it!" Got what? What do you have? One team commits the ultimate sin of letting the ball drop. They all groan while the other side jumps up and down and slaps hands. I take advantage of the break to race into the art room and shut the door behind me. The yelling and squeaking of sneakers on the wood floor fade out immediately. All that's left is the silence of the studio.

I'm totally psyched about this class. I wonder if Ms. Rothstein will remember that she told me about it. I smile at her as I come in, and she does smile back. But not in any big way, like, *Hey, I remember you.*

Which is cool. I get out my sketch pad and take a stool toward the back of the studio. What I really hope is that by the end of the year, I can actually get some-where in my goal to draw people in a way that captures who they are. What they look like. For a second, I think of my portrait of Sari, but I'm not going to work on that. I want to start with something totally fresh and new.

Ms. Rothstein is looking around like she's counting heads. She frowns a little, then goes to the center of the studio, ready to start. Just then, the door swings open and someone comes in. They're late, so everyone in the class turns to see who it is.

I look too.

But I can't believe who it is.

It's David Cole.

For a second, I just stare. It is utterly bizarre to see David Cole. And here, in the art studio. After all this time with Sari, trying to find him, and now here he is, and here I am, and it's like some alternative universe where you go, *Whoa, didn't expect that.*

I mean, soccer guys do not do art. They just don't. I half expect him to say, *Oops. Took a wrong turn,* and leave.

But he doesn't. Instead, he smiles and raises his hand at Ms. Rothstein, like, *Hi.* And then . . . he sits down.

And Ms. Rothstein is smiling at him, like, *Good, now we can start.* Like she was waiting for him, for God's sake.

I cannot believe this. Art. My one refuge, and here's David Cole, strolling into it just because he needs some cheap, easy credits in his last semester in high school. This totally sucks. I feel invaded. Taken over. Like now the thing that's more important to me than anything else in the world will be just another reason for Sari to talk about David, David, David.

I can imagine how Sari will react when I tell her:
Oh, my God.
Tell me everything.
What did he say?
Did he say anything? Anything about me?

Frankly, I don't even feel like telling her. I know I have to. Sari would absolutely want to know this.

But sometimes I wonder: Does everything in my life have to be about what Sari wants?

8

An extremely strange thing happened to me today.

It was in art class. I got there early and picked a seat all the way at the end of one table. With David Cole in the class, I prefer to sit where I won't be noticed. It has been three weeks since Erica's party, and he still hasn't called Sari. I'm beginning to think he's never even going to talk to Sari again. Which is cruel and obscene—and why I don't want to be anywhere near him.

If David knows who I am, if he even remembers who Sari is, he is doing an excellent job of hiding it.

Still.

So, there I am, fiddling with my latest sad attempt, wondering how almost a month can have gone by, and I'm still no better at drawing people, when I am suddenly aware that the stool I'm on has moved. That, in fact, *I* have moved.

And that David Cole is standing right next to me, holding another stool in his hands.

What has happened is this: As David pulled the stool next to mine out from under the table, one of its legs got caught on one of my stool's legs and turned it.

David's frowning down at the stool he's holding. Then he glances over at me.

He says, "Oh, hey. Sorry."

"That's okay."

I say it before I even know I'm saying it. In this voice that does not sound like mine at all. A voice that really doesn't belong to Sari's best friend, to someone who knows for a fact that David is King Scum.

If I could take back that "That's okay," I would. Instead I stare down at my sketch pad. I'm sure David notices me not looking at him.

Out of the corner of my eye, I can see David moving his stool around mine, carefully putting it down a few inches away. Like it matters or something.

He sits. Puts his elbows on the table, folds his hands together. He looks at them like he's worried, like they're stupid and who knows what they'll do next.

Then he looks over at me, kind of smiles, like, *Sorry again.*

And I kind of smile back, like, *It's okay.*

I have not told Sari that David is in my class. She never asks me anything about my art class, what goes on there, what I'm doing. So, so far, it just hasn't come up.

Actually, a lot of the time, I forget I meant to tell her.

For Friday, I have to write an essay for English. Mr. Barry said it could be on anything we wanted. So, here's my essay:

WHY VALENTINE'S DAY SHOULD BE BANNED
by Jesse Horvath

Valentine's Day should be banned. Why? For the following reasons. One, it divides the world into the Haves and Have-Nots of cuteness and popularity. Those without boyfriends or girl-friends are made to feel inferior when they see some idiot running around with a stupid card with a bunny on it saying I WUV YOU. We are forced to endure squeals and giggling and competitive card comparisons. It is a waste of time.

Valentine's Day should also be banned because it promotes the worst aspects of our culture: consumerism and bad taste. There is not a single decent Valentine's Day card. They are all obnoxious and overly pink. Nonetheless, people buy them in huge quantities. Then they just throw them away. These cards are probably not recyclable, and so end up in some landfill, thus further polluting our environment and taking up precious resources.

People buy more chocolate for Valentine's Day than at any other time of the year. Chocolate is full of caffeine and it makes you fat. It is usually imported from poor countries where they are forced to grow cocoa instead of things they need, like wheat.

Pink is one of the world's worst colors. Hearts make me gag.

Next year, I think everyone should just take the money they were going to spend on cards and chocolate and stuffed animals and donate it to some worthy cause.

VALENTINE'S DAY—JUST SAY NO!

Barry gave me a B+. His comments were: *Original and well-constructed essay. Style occasionally burdened by pedantic stridency.*

Okay, even I know that Valentine's Day will never be banned. But in my opinion, the powers that be could at least restrict its observance to the twenty-four hours of February 14. At Eldridge, it's like we've been celebrating it since New Year's. Everywhere you go, there are these revolting hearts on the wall. Little butt-naked cupids swinging from the ceiling. Everyone's eating those candy hearts that say WILL U B MINE? And, of course, they all keep checking their lockers for Valentine's Day cards.

Possibly the only person in a worse mood than me is Sari. That's because we are now on day I-don't-even-know-what, and Cole the Cool still hasn't called.

And now even Sari knows he's not going to.

So that's it. The great love affair of her life is toast.

"Excuse me while I puke."

Sari nods. "Totally."

It is Valentine's Day. The thing that's about to make me puke is the sight of the lockers at Eldridge Alternative. They are fluttering with cards, balloons, teddy bears. Even a school as supposedly hip and cool as Eldridge has its Valentine's traditions. Ours is that you stick the Valentine's card in the door of the beloved person's locker. That way, everyone knows who is seriously popular and who is a hopeless loser.

There's another Eldridge Valentine's Day tradition. That is when you walk by the lockers, you check out the cards, who's got a lot, who's got none. Check out the handwriting, see if you can tell who's sent who a card. Everyone does it. Even I do it. And I—supposedly—couldn't care less.

Sari is an expert. She can identify someone's handwriting with one look. As we're walking past the lockers, she's making comments like, "How sad is Glen Howard having a crush on Amy?" or "I bet Sarah wrote that to herself. Look, you can totally see it's her handwriting."

It's good to see Sari being cruel; for the first time since Erica's party, she sounds like her old self again. I guess I should feel bad that my best friend got dumped by the man of her dreams. But the thing is, if things had turned out differently, the way Sari hoped they would, I might not have my best friend anymore.

We pass by Thea's locker. Sure enough, a billion cards. Sari doesn't have anything to say about that. To distract her, I point out the balloon one of Erica's friends has left on Erica's locker. It's huge and metallic with a big bear on it. I offer to pop it for a dollar. I say, in fact, I will give Sari a dollar if she asks me to pop it. Sari laughs.

We get to our lockers. No valentines on mine, thank God. But someone has left some article about the filming of the *Hollow Planet* movie taped to the door.

"Ooh," says Sari, pointing to the article, "Cupid has struck."

I give her a dirty look. I crumple up the article and throw it in the trash. I know Danny left it. But I no longer acknowledge his existence.

Then I spot something on the floor under Sari's locker. It's a card.

Obviously someone tried to hide it. It's not stuck in the door, it's almost shoved under the locker. Picking it up, Sari turns it over. There's no name on the front.

Sari looks at me. "Should I open it?"

"No, let's just stare at it. *Duh*, Sari."

She starts tearing the envelope. While she does, I think, *Please God, don't let it be from David Cole.*

I look over her shoulder. The card says: *Backstage at Little El. Today. 4:00.*

"Little El" is the Little Eldridge Theater. Backstage is where they keep the chairs and stage flats and a lot of other junk. It is very dark and very hidden. At dances, people go there when they want to be alone.

Sari's looking at the card like it's a letter saying she's won a billion dollars. She gazes and gazes at it, whispering, "I can't believe it. I totally cannot believe it."

I give her a *Wow!* look. Followed by a *So what?* look. I do this because Sari needs me to give her perspective. She is a very perspectiveless person.

Sari doesn't notice. "No way can I wait until four— it's, like, forever."

Here's what I want to ask Sari: *What took him so long? How come he's still hanging around with Thea? Huh? Why is that, if he lo-o-oves you so much?*

Could you please THINK *for one second?*

But all you have to do is look at her face to know that rational thought is no longer an option.

Anyway, maybe he just wants to dump her.

Except I don't really think so.

Half an hour before the Big Rendezvous, Sari drags me into the bathroom. "What do you think?" she asks me. "Do I look okay?"

I nod.

"Really?"

"Sure."

Actually, I don't know what I think. All I know is what Sari wants me to say. So I say it to her.

Sari peers at herself in the mirror. "I am so nervous, I think I'm going to vomit."

"Oh, that's romantic." I look over her shoulder at myself in the mirror. We look like two separate categories of species.

Humanus Sexus. Humanus Uglius.

I mean, I'm not *ugly*. I just don't look like Sari or Erica or Thea or any of the girls who are pretty and hot. I'm extremely ordinary looking. My features would probably look better on a boy. If I were a boy, I would look okay.

I ask Sari, "What do you think's going to happen? What do you think he's going to say?"

Sari catches something in my voice. Looking over her shoulder, she says, "About what?"

About his disappearing act, I'm about to say. But just then, the bathroom door opens and some people come in. Sari tries to look very calm—you know, like she isn't getting ready for the biggest moment of her life. She combs her hair one way, then the other, then runs her fingers through it so it looks like it always does. She runs a lipstick over her mouth, two, three times. Then she stares at herself in the mirror for a long moment, like, *Am I as utterly perfect as I can be?*

Now she's playing with her sweater, pulling it lower. "I wish I'd worn something else. Something that shows *les boobies* more."

I make a face. "Sari."

Grinning, she turns around and shakes them. "Boobs, tits, ta-tas . . ."

"Hello, you're being gross."

"Breast," she says grandly. "Bust. Cleav-age."

"Cleavage?" I laugh. Primarily, because it makes me think of a line from *Hollow Planet: With a single blow, Rana cleaved the enemy's skull like a melon.* You think of breasts as being a pair, but I guess cleavage really means the part in between. The separation.

Sari spins around. "Well?"

"Gorgeous beyond belief," I say.

As soon as we're out of the bathroom, she gives me a quick hug and hurries off. Over her shoulder, she says, "I'll call you later."

I say, "Good luck," but she doesn't hear me.

Which is just as well, because I'm not sure I meant it.

I decide to walk home through the park. I need some time to think.

Kicking leaves and dead branches out of my way, I try to sort out all the voices in my head.

My Nice Self says, *Sari's your friend. You should be happy for her.*

My Rotten Self says, *Yeah, well, guess what? I'm not.*

Why not? The question starts echoing in my head, won't quit until it gets answered.

Why not? Why aren't you happy for Sari? What's wrong with you?

Are you jealous?

No, that is absolutely ridiculous. I am totally not jealous of Sari in any way. What on earth do I care if David Cole likes her? The fact is, David Cole is a jerk.

I think this like I'm saying it out loud, but it sounds wrong. I try it again: *David Cole is a jerk.* But it still sounds strange. False.

The fact is, I'm not so sure David Cole is a jerk.

I mean, he acts like a jerk. A lot. But I'm not so sure that's absolutely who he is.

Which makes no sense at all.

What's better? I ask myself. *Sari going out with the*

David Cole who is a jerk or Sari going out with the David Cole who's not a jerk?

Somehow, the first. Sari going out with the David Cole who's not a jerk makes me feel small and weak and sad for some reason.

The thing is, if Sari starts going with David, she will start being that person I hated so much at Erica Trager's party. And not only would I not want to hang around with that person, but that person would definitely not want to hang around with me.

But does David really like Sari? How can he? Why would he dump Thea Melendez, who is gorgeous and popular and . . . The same questions keep going through my head, like some dumb commercial that comes on every five seconds.

I try to switch my brain off, make it go black like the TV, but it won't turn off. Then all of a sudden, I hear a branch snap behind me, and I become completely still inside.

My mom always tells me to be careful in the park, no matter what time of day. She tells me, "Stay on the path."

I still am on the path, but in this hidden, woodsy area. Look around, all you see are trees. I'm not sure that if I scream, anyone will hear me.

Start walking, I tell myself. *Just start walking.*

Then I hear, "Hey, Jess. Wait up."

I turn. And see Danny.

He's all out of breath. Like he's been chasing me forever.

He pants. "Didn't you hear me calling?"

I shake my head.

He takes a step forward, then stops. He's nervous. He should be.

He says, "So, hey."

I say nothing.

"Haven't really seen you around."

I give him this look, like, *That was not an accident.*

"Well, anyway, I wanted to say I'm sorry. About New Year's. And thanks for . . ." He shrugs. "I don't know."

It occurs to me that Sari never said she was sorry after the party. Instead, she said I shouldn't have left.

I say, "Well, I'm glad you got home all right."

Danny smiles. Really smiles—like it means a lot that I'm not mad at him anymore. And then I figure out something weird: that you can be important to someone who doesn't mean much to you. But that once you find that out—that you mean something to them—it's hard not to feel that they mean something to you.

Which is not to say that Danny isn't still a numbnut. Because he is.

He asks, "Did you get the article I left you? They're filming in Australia."

"I knew that already. After that, I heard they're going to Sri Lanka."

"Really?"

"Uh-huh. For the palace scenes." This is not true. I don't know why it is, I can't resist lying to Danny. Seeing what he'll believe, what I can get away with.

We start walking. It's a nice day, cold but very clear. It's quiet because there aren't a lot of people in the park. Branches and leaves crunch under our feet. You could be in the woods somewhere—as long as you don't look up and see the huge buildings everywhere. It feels a zillion miles away from Eldridge.

As we talk about the movie, I realize that Danny is very comprehensive in his knowledge. He remembers details better than I do. Like I forgot that the director had started out doing Anime, although I pretended I hadn't.

We start talking about classes, who sucks, who's kind of okay. We seriously trash Barry. Danny does an imitation of him, and amazingly, it's not that bad.

I find myself wondering if Danny is a geek only within the Eldridge environs. Like, if the walls have some strange biological effect on him. Then once he's away from Eldridge, he's freed from the evil spell and actually not this horrible, boring guy at all, but someone who's . . . okay.

Before I know it, we're on my block. I say to Danny, "I didn't know you lived around here."

"Oh . . ." Danny looks down the block. "I don't really."

I want to ask why he walked all the way to my house then if he didn't have to.

But I stop myself from asking—just in time.

"Well, anyway . . . thanks." I give him half a wave.

"See you tomorrow." He doesn't wave or move. It's like he's waiting for me to promise that this is, in fact, the case. That he will see me tomorrow.

"Yeah, in English." I cross my eyes, and Danny does his Barry imitation again.

Which makes me laugh.

But he's still just standing there.

I say, "Um, look, you want to come up?"

Danny smiles, half shrugs. "Yeah, sure."

The doorman smiles, tips his hat as we come in. He's surprised, I can tell. He's wondering, *Who's the guy? Where's Sari?* He better not make a joke or I'll kill him.

All the same, it occurs to me that I might not tell Sari about Danny coming over.

I show Danny the kitchen, the living room, the bathroom. Then I let him into my room. For a second, he just stands there with his backpack still over his shoulder, like he's not sure what to do. I wonder if anyone ever let him into their room before.

I'm about to ask him if he wants a soda when he sees something and frowns. Setting his backpack on the floor, he walks over to the wall where I have all my pictures up.

I cannot actually tear them all down in a single second. And I can't really bash Danny unconscious. I want to scream, *Don't look at those, they're crap!* But it's already too late. So I let him look.

He says, "Wow. These are amazing."

I am totally embarrassed. I know I should say thanks, but I'm convinced I will sound ridiculous.

Danny's moving down the line of pictures. He looks at one, then steps back to look at another. "Wow." He keeps saying it. "Wow."

He turns to me. "You're really good."

Now I can say it. "Thanks."

"You could do this for real. I mean it."

I feel myself smile, shrug. "I don't know. Maybe."

"No, really."

I've waited for this my whole life. For someone other than my parents to tell me I'm good. Not just better than most people, but really good. The kind of good that lets you do things. The kind of good that gives you freedom.

It feels as good as I thought it would.

Better.

Now Danny's looking at my drawing of Nomi. I like how I did Nomi. He's turning to look over his shoulder, and he's got this wicked little smile.

Danny says, "Nomi's great."

"Yeah, I love Nomi." I'm not sure: Are we talking about the picture or the character?

I sort of swing my arm toward the picture. "You can have it. If you want."

"Yeah?" Danny looks at me.

"Sure. Anything for a fellow Nomi appreciator."

"That's so great. Thanks."

I go over to the wall and gently unstick the paper. Then I scratch away the glue stick until there's only this faint, faint stain on the corner of the paper. I wish it weren't there. I'd like to give it to Danny perfect.

For a second, I hesitate. What if I never draw another Nomi this good? What if Danny loses it or throws it away? A few years from now, it'll just be a dumb drawing to him. To me, it's something I did. Something I did really well.

Then I remember Danny telling me, "You could do this for real." Someone who gives you something like that, you owe them. I hand him the picture.

Danny holds it carefully, staring down at it. "Thanks."

"You're welcome."

That night, I get out my sketch pad and sit on my bed, propped up by three pillows. I want to try another picture of Nomi, to replace the one I gave Danny. But when I start drawing, it turns into something else entirely, a whole other scene, and I get lost in that. So lost, I don't really hear the phone ring, until my dad yells, "Jess? Sari for you."

I pick up, say, "Okay," and wait for my dad to hang up. When he does, I hear Sari whisper, "Jess?"

"Hey." Then I remember and ask, "How'd it go?" Like I've been waiting all this time for her to call.

"Oh, my God." Sari's so excited, she can hardly breathe.

"Oh, my God, *what*?"

"Oh, my God, everything," she says. "Oh, my God, I'm in love. Oh, my God, he's amazing. Oh, my God, this has been the most incredible day of my entire life."

"What happened?"

"Well . . ." From Sari's voice, I can imagine her in her room. She's on her bed, probably sitting up so she can give me the whole story. "We went to his house."

Sari has been to David Cole's house. I should say, *Wow.* This is a *wow* thing. But somehow, I can't bring myself to say it.

So instead, I say, "Was anybody else there?"

"At his house?"

"Yeah."

"No," Sari coos. "It was just us."

"Wow."

"Definitely wow." She giggles.

"So what then?"

"We talked . . . a lot. And then we played."

From the way she says this, I have to ask, "But you didn't . . . ?"

"What? No. God, I would've told you *that*."

I smile. Good. Sari still thinks it's important to tell me things.

"So, what did he say?"

"Oh, like . . . a million things. We talked about everything."

"Yeah, but . . ." Suddenly I can hear it, like a hum in the silence. *Don't.*

I try to ask nicely. "Was he waiting until Valentine's Day to talk to you?"

There's a long pause. Then Sari says, "You know, I didn't really want to get into it. It doesn't matter now anyway."

Weeks of torment and misery don't matter. Okay.

Sari knows what I'm thinking, because she says quickly, "He said maybe I could come around next Thursday."

"What'd you say?"

"I said yes. What do you think I said?"

I don't say anything.

Then I ask, "So, what happens with Thea?"

"I don't know. We didn't talk about her."

"But she has to know, right?"

"I don't know. Whatever."

"Won't that bug you?"

"No." Sari's voice is definite, like she's been waiting for the question and knows just what to say. "It's totally none of my business."

How do you tell your best friend you think she's lying?

"But there is one thing," says Sari.

One thing? Try a million. "What?"

"You cannot tell anybody about this. About David and me. I mean, nobody."

"I'm not going to."

"I mean it. Not a living soul."

Yeah, I think, *because then a living soul might tell Thea.*

"I won't."

"Swear."

"I swear," I tell her, feeling moronic. "I will tell *no one.*"

There's a long pause while, I guess, Sari tries to decide if I've sworn enough. Then she says, "So, the Book was right. That's kind of cool."

"What'd it say?"

"About someone new in my life, remember?"

"Oh, yeah." I feel tired. Like I don't really want to talk anymore.

Sari asks, "So, uh, what'd you do today?"

I look at the wall where Nomi's picture used to be.

"Nothing."

9

> The Alliance was troubled. The parties were quarreling and fragmented. Rana surveyed the Great Hall frowning. Where would it all lead? How could they hope for victory when they conspired at their own defeat?
>
> —*Hollow Planet: Thorvald's Hammer*

As far as Eldridge Alternative is concerned, David and Thea are still the perfect couple.

They still sit together at lunch. They still grab each other under the table in history class.

Thea ♥ *David* BIG TIME is still on the third-floor bathroom wall.

David still sneaks up on Thea in the hallway. Thea still screams and acts annoyed when he tickles her. She still kisses him and says she forgives him.

David and Sari never, ever speak at school. I don't think they even look at each other.

But every Thursday, after school, they get together at David's house.

And that's how it's been. For almost a month.

It's weird—you look around the lunchroom, and it's like nothing has changed. There's David and Thea and their crew, over at the big table in the corner where they sit whenever they deign to eat in the cafeteria. Near them, there's the Drama-holics, the theater group; over there, the hard-core cyberheads; then the Harvard-bounds—everyone in their own little spot in the universe.

The lowly ninth graders form the outer ring; we get jostled and bumped by everyone looking for a place to sit. Right near us, Erica Trager and her Pradettes are yakking away. They keep looking over at David and Thea's table. No big surprise. That's what David and Thea are for: to be looked at, talked about.

But Erica Trager's not the only one staring at David and Thea. Sari's also got her eyes fixed on them. She has this little smile on her face, like she's the only one who knows how this is all going to turn out.

Here's what I don't get: How can you be madly, psychotically in love with someone and only see them on Thursdays?

How can you stand that they're still seeing someone else?

How can you not feel humiliated?

I'm dying to ask Sari. But I don't dare.

Sari's "in love." And apparently, when you're in love, you don't mind being in love with someone who pretends you don't exist except on Thursdays.

A chubby computer guy trips on his way back to his table, and the soccer crew cracks up laughing. Roaring, clapping, stamping—the whole bit. Their superiority has been vindicated, and they're just way too happy. Sari's smirking too. I want to say to her, *Yeah, you're not sitting over there with them; you're down here with the rest of us freaks and losers.*

I ask her, "What do you guys *do* when you get together?"

She gives me a sly sideways look. "I don't think you want to know. I think you might be shocked."

I roll my eyes. "Well, don't you ever want to do anything else?"

Sari looks scornful. "Like what? Go to a *movie*?" She says this like going to a movie is the most moronic thing you could ever do.

I say, "But doesn't it bug you, watching him and . . ." I nod my head toward Thea.

"No." Sari glances over her shoulder. "I kind of get off on it. It's like a big joke."

Now David has his arm around Thea, and he's chewing on her ear. I know that's supposed to be wildly sexy, but it looks gross to me.

I can't even imagine what Sari feels like, watching this.

I say, "We can go if you want to."

Sari laughs, says, "Puh-leeze."

"Puh-leeze" is Sari's new favorite word. It's something Thea and her friends say.

David is still crawling all over Thea. Thea shrieks, pretends to push him away. ". . . all *hands*, my God."

He grabs for her hair, but she pushes him away again. This time, it seems like she means it.

And Sari just keeps smiling.

While all this is going on, I keep my head down, pretending to be insanely involved in my book. I don't think David notices me sitting next to Sari, and I don't want him to. I don't know why, but I don't.

Well, I do know why. Partly. It's because of what happened last week in art class.

But that's not something I want to think about right now.

I still haven't told Sari about it.

When it's time for class, we get up and walk out of the lunchroom. Sari picks up her bag. It's new, a Tornado.

I head directly for the door. But Sari deliberately walks around David's table so that he has to see her. I stand by the exit and wait for her to catch up. I notice: When Sari walks by, David doesn't even see her; he keeps right on talking to his friends.

Once she sees he's not looking, Sari speeds up a little. She has this look on her face, and I can tell she's upset.

We leave the lunchroom, and Sari doesn't say anything. She just stares straight ahead, biting her lip.

It's sort of hard to look at her; I keep thinking of what I want to say, and I'm scared it'll show on my face.

I want to say: *Stop deluding yourself.*

I want to say: *It's his stupid game. Stop playing it.*

Sari sighs, shifts her Tornado bag to the other shoulder. I want to give her something, make her remember she has a life all the time, not just on Thursdays.

As we walk up the stairs, I say, "Hey, *Bloodsuckers* opens on Friday."

Sari raises her eyebrows, says, "Hmm."

"From the commercials, it looks seriously bad. Definite cheesy effects." We swing around the landing. Sari goes first, and I follow her up. "I think it may have to be seen."

"I don't know."

"Come on—so bad, it's good." I'm about to remind her of *The Worm*, a movie we saw last year that was so truly, truly bad we both fell out of our chairs, we laughed so hard. We could hardly walk home. We kept shrieking, "The worm! The worm!" and cracking up.

I'm just about to say, *The worm! The worm!* when Sari says, "I don't know if bad movies are tops on my list of life experiences."

I joke, "Are you kidding? They're essential life experiences."

But Sari doesn't get it. Instead, she looks annoyed. Not like she looked annoyed at David, but something else.

In this tight voice, she says, "Yeah, well . . ." She shoves the door to the third floor open, says, "Maybe not to everyone, you know?"

Sari goes through the door, and before it swings shut, I follow. Sari doesn't look back, just keeps heading down the hall. And after a while, I stop trying to keep up and let her go.

I have a few minutes before class, so I sit in the third stall of the bathroom and think.

First I let my brain empty out completely, until all I know is blankness.

Then I let in the image of Sari pushing the door, let the words "Yeah, well . . . Maybe not to everyone" echo for a while.

Then I think of her walking by David's table, think of her face when he didn't look up.

And what I decide is this:

David is treating Sari really, really badly.

And that's why she's in such a crummy, insecure mood.

I don't think she would have been so nasty otherwise.

I really don't.

I mean, I couldn't deal with what she's dealing with.

Not that I'll probably ever have to.

The fact is, I have a nervous breakdown exchanging three words with David Cole.

That's not my imagination; it's the truth.

I know because now I have actually exchanged three words with David Cole.

It's not that big a thing.

But it's not a nothing thing, either.

If that makes any sense.

For the past few weeks, ever since he bumped my chair, I always end up sitting at the same table with David Cole in art class. I do not plan this. He always sits at the same table I do. I have no idea why.

It was the day we were doing eyes. You'd think by now that I'd have, like, a hundred portraits, but I don't. So far, all I have is body parts, because that's all Ms. Rothstein's let us do. I have page after page of noses. Two whole pages of ears. Three and a half of mouths.

I could tell David was having a hard time. Not that

I spend my whole time staring at him, but I noticed he kept putting his pencil down and sighing. At one point, he even tried to look over at what I was doing, but I put my arm around my sketch pad so he couldn't see.

Then I heard him say, "You know what? Eyes are a complete drag."

Even though that was about the dumbest thing I'd ever heard, I knew someone would agree with it, because people love to agree with David Cole. I waited for whoever he was talking to to say, *Yeah, right, man.*

But no one did. Then I looked up and saw he was talking to me.

"Don't you think?" He grinned. "I mean, they're not like *nostrils.* Nostrils are cool. They're the best."

I said, "Nah, earlobes."

I absolutely did not mean to say it. But it's like I forgot who I was talking to—I guess because I never thought David Cole would make something as geeky as a nostril joke.

"Earlobes are okay too." He pointed at me. "You drew a seriously good ear last week."

I shrug. It was a good ear. Very twisty and cavernous, closed and open at the same time.

Then he held up his pad, showed me his eyes. "So, what do you think?"

I tried to keep from wincing. Frankly it wasn't much. Just two bow shapes connecting, with a lot of wild lines for lashes.

After a moment, I said, "You need the inside part." He frowned, and I pointed to my own eye. "You know, the . . ." Then I held up my drawing and showed him. "This part."

I had done these two enormous eyes that filled the entire page. If you look at them long enough, you feel almost hypnotized by them. I have to confess, I think they're quite cool.

Looking at the eyes, David Cole's own eyes got wide. Like he was imitating them.

"That's really something," he said, but in his Cool Dude voice, a kind of dry drawl that sounds like he'll crack up laughing any second because you're so slow, you take him seriously.

I knew not to take him seriously and went back to my work.

I heard him say, "Come on, I mean it."

I shook my head. Because that's how they get you: pretend to be nice, then make you hurt.

"Hey . . ." I felt my sketch pad tug away from my fingers, so I had to look up. Right into David Cole's face. "I'm serious, okay?"

He grinned, gave me back the pad. "But you can't take me seriously all the time."

Not looking at him, I said, "Yeah, believe me, I don't."

He laughed. "Cool with me."

Then he went back to his work. "Cool with me."

There is no way I could tell Sari any of this. She would just say it's because I'm her friend, that that's why David is nice to me. And I would have to tell her that that's not true. Because I honestly don't think David Cole remembers that I am Sari's friend.

At any rate, he has never once mentioned her to me.

As I leave the bathroom, I have this vision: Sari, David, and Thea go on one of those shows where everyone screams and throws chairs and the audience claps for their favorite. The show could be on "Guys Who Cheat and Women Who Love Them," but they could tell Thea it was about something else, like "Perfect High School Couples."

I don't think I could ever be on a show like that. I'm not crazy or dumb enough. Plus, I think you have to wear a miniskirt, and I don't have one.

I would be in the studio audience.

Because of my meditation session in the bathroom, I am now late for my next class, which is math.

My dad says it's lame to hate math. But I have sound, logical reasons for hating it. For one thing, I am not good at it. (Dad says this is because I have decided to hate it, but he's wrong.) For another, this year, freshman algebra is taught by Bernard McGuiness, who has an unnervingly long nose hair and smells strange.

But thirdly, I have the same math class as Erica Trager and her Pradettes. Which makes me feel like I have been banished to the very lowest circles of hell.

I always try to get to math early, so I can sit as far away from Erica and her cronies as possible. But by the time I get there, every single seat is taken—except for one, right next to guess who.

I'm pretty sure that prolonged exposure to the toxin that is Erica Trager is a definite health risk, but the fact is, I don't really have a choice. So I sit down next to her.

Erica, of course, doesn't even notice. She's all busy

yakking to Michelle Burke about some vitally important thing that happened to her over the weekend. It's
weird—for girls who are supposedly so cool, all they do
is talk to each other. If you listen, it isn't even talk.
They just make noises, like, "No" and "I'm saying" and
"Totally." They're like a bunch of orangutans—except
not as cute or smart.

I get out my notebook and start writing *Erica
Trager sucks* over and over. I try not to listen, but it's
impossible. It must be something pretty spectacular
in the world of Erica, because she's leaning in close to
Michelle and whispering intensely, like she's passing
state secrets or something.

"And the thing is—"

Michelle interrupts her. "Oh, I know . . ."

"No, but the thing is . . . she told him that, after
graduation . . ."

"After graduation . . . ?" Michelle prompts her.

I slow down writing. I'm not entirely sure why. But
something tells me to listen.

"After graduation, she wants, you know, some promise"—Erica looks over her shoulder at Mr. McGuiness
to make sure he's not looking over here—"that they'll
stay together. But David . . ."

I stop writing altogether. My pen just stops dead on
the tail of the first "s" in "sucks."

Michelle gasps. "No!"

"Yes. And they have been fighting about it.
Constantly."

Then Michelle forgets to whisper and says in a normal voice, "Oh, my God. So, what . . . ?"

And suddenly, Mr. McGuiness appears at our table and asks Michelle if she has something she'd like to share with the class.

Michelle says no.

Then Mr. McGuiness asks Erica if she would like to solve the problem on the board.

Normally, I would enjoy watching Erica try to pretend she has a clue how to figure out the circumference of a circle. But right now, my mind's on other things.

Like Sari, David, and Thea.

Sari will flip when she hears David and Thea are fighting. She will be thrilled. According to Sari, David + Thea fighting=David + Sari in love.

But I'm not so sure it does.

The thing is, you can't believe everything you hear from Erica Trager. As I've said, she's one of those people who's always talking about somebody, probably because there's nothing she can say about herself. (*Hi, I'm Erica. I'm a jerk.*) She's obsessed with Thea Melendez because she wants to be Thea Melendez, and she's always pretending to "know" everything about everybody.

It occurs to me that I am the only one, aside from Sari and David, who knows that any of this is going on.

That David Cole is fooling around with Sari Aaronsohn every Thursday is something that a lot of people would like to know. It's sick, when you think about it. But the fact is, I could be popular overnight, just from knowing this. And somehow, when I look at Erica and the Prada Mafia and know that I know something they don't, that makes me feel . . . well, powerful.

I think maybe I should ask my parents to let me transfer. Eldridge is definitely warping me.

By the end of the day, I am really feeling like I want to be home. As I head to my locker, I think about how I will go to the kitchen, get a soda, some popcorn, and just go to my room and shut the door.

I think about being on my bed, the radiator rattling, my feet shoved under the blankets. Maybe I'll draw, maybe I'll fall asleep. Nobo will try and jump on the bed. I'll probably let him.

Quiet will be very good.

On my locker, there's a note. Opening it, I can see it's from Danny.

I feel a squiggle of guilt. Ever since that time he came to my house, it's been weird to see him at school. Like here, he's supposed to be Nerdboy Danny. But now that I know he's not, I don't exactly know how to act around him. I keep meaning to ask him if he wants to do something sometime, but I never quite get around to it. And whenever I see him, I'm always scared he's going to ask me if I want to do something.

The note says: *I found the perfect place in my room for Nomi. I put it right next to my desk. I am keeping it very safe, because I'm sure it'll be worth something someday!*

I smile. For no reason, I think of David Cole telling me not to take him seriously, but that he was serious about liking my work.

I like people liking me like this. It's a lot better than . . .

I can't think of what exactly. But I have an image of

Sari giggling next to David at Erica Trager's party. It's definitely better than that.

"Hey."

I look up and see Sari. She's smiling, so I guess she's not mad at me anymore.

She asks, "What are you doing right now?"

I think of my bed, the popcorn, and quiet. "Um, nothing, really."

"Want to go somewhere?"

Sari's eyes are bright, excited. She's rocking on the balls of her feet. What ever it is she's got planned, she's psyched about it.

And I guess I like it that she wants me to do something exciting with her. Because I say, "Sure."

"Cool." She nods, then sees the note. "What's that?"

"Uh, nothing." I shove the note in my pocket. "Something from Danny."

"Oh, God." Sari groans while she pulls on her coat. "Spare us the attentions of Nerdboys. What did it say?"

"No big thing."

"Oh, puh-leeze." Sari shrugs her Tornado bag onto her shoulder.

Then looking back at me, she says, "You do know he has the saddest crush on you."

I say, "He does not." And wonder why I feel like my best friend has just insulted me.

Sari doesn't tell me where we're going. But it doesn't take too long to figure out that we're headed to the park.

They have soccer practice in the park. After school on Mondays, Wednesdays, and Fridays.

It's Monday.

With David Cole and his friends on the team, practice is almost as big a deal as games. A lot of people show up to hang out on the wall and watch. And on Fridays, they all go to McClaren's, where they supposedly sell you beer if you have a fake ID.

It's a very cliquey thing. No Undesirables allowed, just the Chosen Few.

Definitely no ninth graders are allowed.

As we get closer, I start worrying what Sari has planned. There's no way I'm going to tell her about David and Thea fighting. She's the one who used the words "mad" and "psychotic" to describe how she felt about David, and I don't think you tell things like this to a mad, psychotic person.

As we wait for the light to change so we can cross over to the wall, I ask Sari, "What are we doing?"

"Nothing," she says innocently.

"What if Thea's there?"

Sari snorts. "She has tutoring. For calculus. She keeps telling everyone she's dyslexic. She's not dyslexic, she's just dumb."

Thea may not be there, but her friends are. Naturally, they've taken all the best spots on the wall, so Sari and I have to sit way down at the end. From where we are, we can hear them giggling and talking. Every once in a while, one of them will get excited and shriek, "Oh, my God" or "No!"

And, of course, every time David Cole does something—makes a pass, scores a goal—they all cheer.

But so does Sari.

Really loud. Clapping and everything.

So loud that people turn around and notice.

David gets the ball. He streaks toward the goal, slides and shoots the ball in. The guys on the field, the girls on the wall, everyone explodes. David leaps up from the ground, and his teammates gather around him, whooping and cheering. You can tell he loves it. He punches the air at the poor dumb goalie, yelling, "Yeah, yeah!"

Sari lets out a whoop and raises her fists in the air. Three girls with perfect hair turn to glare at her.

Sari pretends not to see them. But I glare back.

For so long that they finally look away.

I look back at the game. Everyone's rushing around after the ball, kicking at each other for control. From down the wall I hear, "Get it, get it!" Then I hear someone laugh, and I know they're laughing at us.

These people think wherever they are, it's their personal territory. Like it's their right to sit on this wall and we have no right at all to be here. Like we're invading their sacred space or something.

I want to yell at them: *I don't want to be here. I don't care about your ridiculous games, or how outrageously cool you are, or whatever power you think you possess. Please do not make the mistake of thinking I do.*

Out loud I say, "God, they're obnoxious."

Sari doesn't look away from David. "Who?"

"Them." I nod back at the girls. "All of them." I mean the jerks on the soccer field, too. Including David Cole.

"Oh." Sari shrugs. "Who cares?"

"*They* do. They think they own this wall, like we don't have a right to be here."

Sari sighs. "You know what? Just . . . chill."

I stare at her. "What do you mean?"

For a second, Sari doesn't say anything, and I think she's going to apologize, say she didn't mean it.

But she says, "I mean, it's not like you know any of these people, and I just think you should chill out about them. I mean, why do you care?"

Her voice is very forceful, like she's been wanting to say this for a long time. But she doesn't have the nerve to look me in the face.

I say, "I don't care all that much."

"Then why do you talk about them all the time?"

"I don't talk about them all the time."

"Yes, you do."

She thinks she's being so strong, I can tell. Telling me the truth. She's looking at me now, so sure she's right.

I think: *I hate you.*

I want to say: *The reason we talk about "them" all the time is because you're always talking about David. And the reason you're always talking about David is because, secretly, you just want to be one of "them." And what makes it even worse is that I don't think you like David that much, you're just all hot about what he represents, the cool ones, the Exalted Ones. . . .*

But before I can say any of this, Sari blurts out, "They're just people, you know? So what if they care about what they wear? So what if they have money and they haven't read every book under the sun—that doesn't make them evil, you know? People just get so jealous of them, it makes me sick."

I don't say anything. Everything I think of is too violent, too final. I don't even feel like I know Sari anymore. This girl sitting next to me, cheering a bunch of airhead soccer players like they mean something . . .

I count to two hundred.

Then I say I have to go home.

As I walk away, I want to look back to see Sari's face. See if she's even noticed I'm gone.

But that would be weak. And I am not weak.

Sari is.

But I'm not.

10

> The attack would be swift, merciless.
> The key objective—a victory that would
> send a terrible message to the enemy:
> We are more powerful than you
> dreamed. Fear us.
>
> —*Hollow Planet: Desert of Souls*

It's 11:30, and I know for a fact that time has stopped.
The clock will never move again. I am stuck in French
class forever, for the rest of my life.

Madame Balmain is asking me something. Unfortunately, she's asking it in French, which I don't speak.
What she's asking me sounds sort of like, *Would you like
to kill the big stupid cat?* But I know she can't be asking
me that, so I just say, *"Non, merci."*

She raps her knuckles on the desk. *"Non, merci?"*

Non, merci beaucoup? I don't know. I try to give this
very French shrug. Madame Balmain sighs and says,

"Lea . . ." She repeats the question—which still sounds to me like, *Would you like to kill the big stupid cat?* And Lea says, *Yes, I would like to kill the big stupid cat on Wednesday, thank you very much.*

There is only one way to restore the flow of time to the universe. I raise my hand and ask to go to the bathroom.

Madame Balmain is probably hoping I never come back. She's probably hoping I just disappear into some Spanish class and never darken her *porte encore.*

Walking right out of the building wouldn't be the worst idea.

It wouldn't be the best idea, either.

There's no one else in the bathroom, so I figure I can sit here for five minutes, until the universe gets moving again and shoves that second hand forward. I sit in the middle stall and have a look at what Eldridge is up to.

And that's when I see it.

On the wall, someone has written:

Top Ten Eldridge Sluts

Alex Harding is number one. That's not a huge surprise. Alex makes a thing of going for guys on the wrestling team. I don't know, but from what I hear, guys on wrestling teams aren't really big on hand holding and pecks on the cheek.

But here's the thing: Sari is number two.

The handwriting on the two names is different. So someone started with the obvious—Alex—and then someone else added Sari.

Thea, it has to be Thea. Or one of her friends, someone who saw Sari at the wall.

There are a few other names on the list. Someone wrote

Mr. Barry, which is good, and Melissa Goldfarb, which is really mean, because Melissa's ugly and very shy and couldn't be a slut even if she wanted to. They even wrote *ha, ha* afterward. Just so you get how hilarious the joke is.

I look at Sari's name again. Whoever wrote it used a purple fine-point pen. I try to remember if I have ever seen Thea use a purple pen, but I don't have any classes with her, so I have no way of knowing. But it doesn't look like Thea's handwriting. It doesn't look like Her, if you know what I mean. This handwriting is all scripty and cutesy, like the person might have made a heart on the "i" of Sari's name—that is, if they weren't calling her a slut. Thea doesn't seem like a heart-on-the-"i" type of person.

I wonder if Sari has seen this.

I don't think so.

For one thing, if she had seen it, she would have written something back.

Sari will freak. The thing about being called a slut, it's not so much about what you're doing, it's about how you're doing it. There's a basic difference between girlfriends and sluts. Girlfriends are chosen.

Sluts are stupid.

Sluts give it up to guys who don't care about them.

Sluts get used.

I better wipe Sari's name off before she sees it.

I take some toilet paper and spit on it. But just before I start rubbing at her name, I stop. Something about this feels wrong. I look up at the bathroom wall. Tons of stuff is scribbled all over it, in pencil, in ballpoint pen, in felt-tip pen. This is one place you're allowed to say anything you want. The rule is: You see something you don't like, you write something back.

But you don't wipe it off.

Ever.

Without thinking, I crumple the paper in my hand. Maybe Sari should see this.

I leave the bathroom the way it was when I came in.

At lunch, I look around the lunchroom for Sari and her dumb Tornado bag. Not that I would sit with her if I saw her, but for some sick reason, I want to know if she's here. If she'll come over if she sees me.

But she's not here, so I'll never know.

Danny's not here either. Since the two humans who would deign to be seen in my presence are absent, I'm doomed to eat lunch by myself.

Which is okay, I tell myself. I have done it before. I have survived.

But I'm just taking *Cinescape* magazine (required literature for all sci-fi addicts and other maladjusts) out of my bag when I sense a distinctly alien presence nearby.

I look up and see Erica Trager standing near my table.

Like it isn't a mistake. Like she wants to be there.

She even smiles at me. Which nearly makes me lose my lunch.

"Hi."

I do not owe Erica Trager anything good. So I see no reason to say hi back.

"No Sari today?" Erica Trager has this gross, chirpy little voice that makes her sound like a psychotic doll. Instead of "Ma-ma," it says, "Pra-da." It cannot be natural; she must choose to talk this way.

I say, "No, no Sari today."

"Just . . . you always eat lunch with her, right? Like, I always see you together."

Erica Trager knows I eat lunch with Sari. Erica Trager knows who I am? Alternative universe time.

I say, "She's busy preserving rats' brains in formaldehyde."

This is absolutely not true. But I figure it will disgust Erica Trager.

I figured right. Erica wrinkles her perfect, probably surgically altered nose like she's going to vomit, which would be most excellent, all over her Prada shoes.

Then she says, "Well, you're just a really good friend to her, that's all I can say."

And she walks away.

For about three seconds, I think of following her and making her tell me what she meant by that. But I don't. First, because I'm not sure that Sari and I will ever eat lunch together again, and second, because Erica Trager and I are members of different species, and I can't still quite believe that we had an actual conversation.

After lunch, I find a note on my locker. A piece of paper folded over with my name on it.

Before I open it, I think what it might be:

Dear Ms. Horvath,
    You are just too strange to attend Eldridge Alternative. Please leave the building at once and never return.
                Sincerely,
                Jeannie Carsalot
                a.k.a. Gee-She-Farts-a-Lot

Dear Jess,

David and I are running off together. We are going to get married and have a million children—all of them named David.

> *Your former friend,*
> *Sari*

P.S. Please pass this note to Thea.

The message is from Sari. But that's not what it says. It says: *Meet me on the wall after school. We must talk!*

Which means only one thing: Sari has definitely seen what's on the third-floor girls' bathroom wall.

At first, I think the best thing would be not to go. Just let Sari wait until she figures out I'm not coming.

I imagine her sitting there, getting colder and colder, frowning and wondering where I am. Wondering why I haven't rushed to her side, panting, *Ooh, ooh, Sari, what's happened? Ooh, ooh, please tell me.*

Wondering if maybe she was a jerk and that's why I'm not there.

This is what I'm thinking as I'm walking to the park, not really admitting to myself that I'm going. Part of me really wants to turn around, say, *Screw it*, and never see Sari again.

But then I do see her. Across the street, sitting cross-legged on the wall. And then she sees me and starts waving like a madwoman, and I have no choice anymore.

She's smoking a cigarette, something she does only when she's seriously upset. And never around me, because she knows cigarette smell makes me puke.

She says, "Did you see it?"

I don't know what to say. I get up on the wall next to her.

Sari says, "You saw it, right?"

"That stupid list?"

Sari nods. Her mouth is really tight. Her whole body looks like she wants to hit something.

I think: *I should have wiped her name off. I am a rotten friend.*

"I know who it was," she says. "Who wrote it. I totally know who it was."

"Who?"

"Give me a break. It was Thea."

I'm a little surprised that Sari's so sure. "You recognize the handwriting?"

"I don't have to. I just know it was her."

Sari lights up another cigarette. "Well, the joke's on her, because here's what I'm going to do." She takes a deep drag. "I'm going to tell David he's got to choose. Her or me."

I turn and look at Sari. "Really?"

"Mm-hmm."

"Wow."

I can't believe she's finally going to say it. I can't believe she's willing to risk it. I mean, she has to know if she pushes David to choose, he'll pick Thea.

I feel a rush of excitement that feels weirdly like happiness. And it's not just that it's always cool when something real is about to happen. It's because I know that once David says, *No*—once he says, *Are you crazy?*—then Sari will see.

She'll see that she'll never belong. That they'll never let her because any outsider threatens their power. And once she sees that, she'll be the Sari she used to be. My friend.

I ask, "When?"

"Right after this. When I get home, I'm going to call him."

I ask, "Will David do it?"

"He better."

"But what if he doesn't?"

Sari shrugs. "Then I guess we move on to step two."

I guess: "You tell Thea."

Sari nods.

Then she says, "Not that I want to do that." She's practicing, I can tell, for how she'll say that to David. Swing the leg, fiddle with her sweater, look down at the ground. *Of course, I don't want to do that, David.*

"But you think he will dump her?" What I'm trying to get here is: *Has he ever told you he would?* Because this is too important; I have to know.

Sari makes a face. "I'm not sure. He's totally gutless when it comes to her. It's pathetic the way he jumps when she speaks. 'Oh, David?' 'Yes, dear?' 'Lick my shoe.' 'Of course, darling.'"

I laugh.

Sari frowns. "I don't even know why I love him so much."

I keep quiet.

Sari gives a big sigh. "But I do. And believe me, Thea is going to be seriously sorry she screwed with me." She grins. "Can you imagine if, at the senior party,

David comes with me and Thea has to be there all by her sorry self?"

"She'd be really upset."

Sari laughs. "Excellent. It'll be *excellent*."

She laughs again, then stops. Almost like she laughed because she didn't know what else to do.

For a while, we both watch our feet swing against the stone. Somehow, talking about Thea has left us with nothing else to say to each other.

Then I hear Sari say, "Uh, you know, yesterday?"

"Forget it, it doesn't matter." It does matter. But I couldn't stand it if Sari says the wrong thing, like it was my fault too. If she does feel like that, I'd rather not ever know.

"I was a jerk."

Instantly, I say, "You weren't a—"

Then I see she's smiling.

"Okay, maybe a tiny little bit of a jerk."

Sari picks at her fingernail. "I don't know, for some reason, I felt like you were judging me. And you're the only person I can talk to about this, so, I don't know, I just freaked out."

It's funny with Sari. Just when you think she isn't paying attention, she doesn't have a clue what's going on in your head, she shows you how wrong you are.

I think: *She knows me really, really well.*

I say, "I was judging them, not you. You're totally different from them."

She nods. "No, I know. Just . . . what you think . . . is really important to me." She looks me in the eye. "You know?"

I swallow. "Same here."

"I mean it. There's no one else I would ever trust with this. If I didn't have you as a friend, I think I'd go totally nuts."

I say, "You are nuts."

"Yeah, well, so are you."

"That's probably why we're friends."

"Probably."

For an hour, we sit there on the wall. We talk about what will happen, what David will say, what Sari will say back. Despite what I said, Sari is right. I did judge her. And I feel pretty rotten about that, particularly now, when we're getting along like nothing weird ever happened.

I wish I could hang out with her much longer, but I can't because it's a school night.

Jumping down from the wall, I say, "Call me. When it's over."

She nods. "Absolutely."

And we wave good-bye.

As I walk home, I can't believe how much better today feels than yesterday.

Later that night, after dinner, my dad and I are clearing the table when the phone rings. I know it's Sari. Immediately, I put the stack of plates down and say, "I'll get it."

I grab the kitchen phone, say hello. Sari says, "It's me."

I tell my dad: "I'm going to take it in my room."

When I get to my room I yell, "Okay." Then I wait

until I hear my dad hang up in the kitchen. Then I tell Sari it's okay, go ahead.

She says, "I did it. I talked to him."

"And?"

For a long time, Sari doesn't say anything. Then I hear, "I told him I thought it was time to . . . change things."

"And what did he say?"

"Um . . . he said he thought things were okay the way they were." There's a long silence after that. Sari's whispering, so her parents don't hear. But even over the phone, I can hear that she's at least thinking about crying. Or she has cried and doesn't want to start again.

"So, what'd you say?"

"I told him that I didn't agree."

"And?"

"He said he needed to think about it. How he's been going out with Thea for a really long time and how it wouldn't be fair to her and—"

I say, "Well, this isn't fair to you."

Sari doesn't say anything.

Finally, I say, "I just don't think he's being very nice to you."

Sari sighs. "I know, but . . ."

But what? I want to ask her. I don't get it. How can Sari be so tough and so confident before she talks to David and so scared and weird after she talks to him?

"Did you tell him you'd tell Thea?"

There's a long pause. Then Sari says, "I thought I'd save that. Like if he says, 'I've thought about it and, no,' then I'll say, 'Fine, we're over, and I'm off to tell Thea.'"

"Did he say when he would decide?"

"No. I didn't think it would be too cool to pressure him."

I don't know what to say.

"It is a big thing," she says, suddenly all defensive. "I mean, when you've been going out with someone a long time."

Translation: *Which you wouldn't understand, since you never have and probably never will go out with someone.*

For a while, neither one of us says anything. In the silence, I shout at Sari in my head. *You used to be the bravest person I knew. You would do anything. Say anything. And now you're afraid to stand up to this guy who treats you like dirt?*

Oh, and by the way, you used to be a great friend. But lately, you've been a major cow.

Sari says, "If he thinks about it and says no, then I'll tell Thea."

I listen hard, trying to hear if she means it or not.

She says, "I won't put up with that. I'm not just going to be dumped like that."

I still can't tell if she's trying to convince me or herself. I say, "Okay."

She laughs. "Come on, you know me. I have no mercy."

And I laugh too. That does sound like the old Sari.

I just hope it really is.

11

> With a deafening explosion, the battle was joined.
>
> —*Hollow Planet: Thorvald's Hammer*

It's been three weeks since Sari told David he had to break up with Thea. Three weeks since he said he would think about it.

Guess what? He's still thinking about it.

I mean, I guess he's still thinking about it. Sari hasn't actually said anything. And I think she would have told me if David had said to her, *I am dumping Thea. It's you I love.*

Here's the thing: If someone's madly, psychotically in love with you, it doesn't take them three weeks to figure it out.

I can't say this to Sari. She doesn't need me hurting her feelings.

But I don't think she's going to the senior party.

Everybody's talking about the senior party these days. It's the biggest event of the year. It happens the day before graduation, and it goes on all night, with everybody drinking and dancing until dawn. It's always held at a secret, undisclosed location. Only three kinds of people are permitted to know where it is. They are:

a. Seniors

b. Cool people

c. People who date one of the above

Now, anybody can crash. But you have to know where it is and be cool enough that you won't immediately get thrown out. So everybody's trying to figure out where it might be or who they can get to invite them.

One day, I'm putting my books away in my locker when I hear some girl talking about it. She's behind me, and I don't see who she is. I don't immediately recognize her voice, but I don't not recognize it, either, if you know what I mean. I start to half listen.

"Yeah, he's already bitching and moaning about having to go, but I was, like, 'Honey, if I'm organizing it, you are going to be there.'"

And then someone else says, "Have you guys found a place?"

"We're looking at some lofts downtown, but they all want a bajillion dollars."

Carefully, I shut the door to my locker and turn in the direction of the voices.

I was right. It's Thea.

She and her friend have stopped to get a drink of water. Thea's leaning against the wall, while her friend drinks from the fountain. Thea's, like, two feet away from me.

For some reason, I suddenly feel horribly guilty. Which is dumb. I haven't done anything to Thea.

"David says he doesn't want to go to any parties at all. He'd rather we just take off someplace by ourselves."

The friend giggles. "Ooh."

I think: *This is not good for Sari. This is not good at all.*

Then, as they get ready to move on, Thea looks over in my direction. She smiles, frowns a little, like she knows she's seen me but can't remember who I am.

Then she drops the frown and smiles full out. She says, "Hey," but not because she really knows me.

I say, "Hey" back. But quietly.

Because I just found out something I didn't want to know.

Thea's not an evil person. In fact, she's kind of nice.

And David definitely has not dumped her.

I wonder if Sari knows. I have a feeling she might. I have a feeling that David hasn't called her, and she knows that means he made a choice—and it's not her.

But why hasn't she said anything?

I wonder if she thinks I'm sick of it. That I don't want to hear it anymore.

Which means she's feeling rotten all by herself.

I should let her know it's okay if she wants to talk about it.

Later, when I meet up with Sari for lunch, I ask, "So, any interesting phone calls lately?"

Sari says, "From who?"

"You know."

Sari frowns, like she really can't figure it out. Then she nods. "Oh. You know, I don't want to talk about it. It's like . . . getting obsessive already. He'll call when he calls."

She sounds all offhand about it, like she couldn't care less. Sometimes she'll do this, say she doesn't want to talk about something—but then she always ends up going back to it. She can't help herself.

But not this time. Now she's going on and on about her Spanish class, and how she doesn't know how she's going to pass because she knows, like, two words of Spanish, *hola* and *gracias.* And for some strange reason, I feel disappointed. Not that I want Sari to keep going on and on about David Cole, but now that she won't talk about it, I feel . . . wrong somehow. Like it's a dis on me, not David.

Which is ridiculous. And pathetic on my part. If Sari's trying to get over David, the last thing I should do is bug her to talk about him.

As we're leaving the cafeteria, I say, "Hey, you want to hang out sometime this week? Do a movie maybe?"

Sari smiles. "Yeah, cool."

"Maybe Thursday."

For a second, Sari hesitates. I guess it's hard to think about No More Thursdays with David. But then she says, "Yeah, Thursday's good."

"Maybe even . . . *Bloodsuckers*?"

"No! Definitely not *Bloodsuckers*." Sari laughs. "Oh, okay, maybe."

I want to hug her for being so brave, for saying she'll see *Bloodsuckers*, for being such an ultimately cool human being. But instead, I just promise her *Bloodsuckers* will be a peak cultural experience, one she will not regret.

We're walking up the stairs. Sari stops at the third floor, while I keep heading up to five. She gives me a questioning look, and I point upstairs. "Art."

"Oh, right." Sari nods.

There's this pause, and I feel like now, today of all days, she's going to ask me something about my class. I can't believe I never told her David was in the class. It's been so long, I've forgotten it was something I was keeping a secret from her.

I bite my tongue, a reminder to myself not to say anything.

But all Sari does is open the door and give a little wave good-bye. "Okay, see ya."

"Yeah, see ya."

This time when I get to class, David's already sitting at the table in the back. Normally, I would just go sit at my regular place at the end of the table. But today, I stop. Today, I'm not going to sit next to David Cole like he didn't do anything wrong, like he didn't hurt anyone.

Instead, I sit at the table right near the front. The girl I sit next to looks at me like, *What are* you *doing here?*

Ms. Rothstein claps her hands to get our attention. When she has it, she says, "Today is a special day. Today, we begin our first full portrait."

Everyone in the class starts clapping and cheering. Including me. Finally, we get to do a real, whole face. I make a big symbolic turn to a fresh page in my pad. I'm totally psyched. At last, I get to finish my Sari portrait. It's been bugging me all year—somewhere, I still have that old squiggle drawing. *And* it's the perfect time to give it to her. Sari loves anything that has to do with how she looks.

I imagine handing it to her, saying, *Here, I thought you might like this.* Or, *Hey, recognize this person?*

Now Ms. Rothstein is going around the room, handing something out. I half rise off my stool, trying to see what it is.

"Ah-ah," she says. "No peeking, Jess."

Then she leans over and gives me . . .

A mirror.

Ms. Rothstein turns around and raises her hand. "I should correct something I said earlier. Today, we begin not just a portrait, but a *self*-portrait."

The whole class groans.

I can't believe this. Every drop of excitement I felt about my first portrait is gone. I can't believe we don't even have a choice, that we *have* to draw ourselves. I have zilch interest in drawing my face. It's dull, boring. Some eyes, a nose, a mouth, pressed into a blah, blobby dough.

Quickly I hold the mirror up, and two narrowed eyes and some ugly teeth flash out at me. *Me,* I think, and put the mirror facedown. Then, without thinking, I glance over at David.

He's got his mirror facedown too.

That night, I get out my sketch pad and sit cross-legged in front of my closet, which has a mirror on the door. I look down at the blank page, then whip my head really fast, eyes open wide.

I'm trying to surprise myself. So I can catch the way I look to other people. It doesn't work. All I see is a staring lunatic in the mirror.

I think I may hate Ms. Rothstein.

Okay, okay. Elements. Eyes, ears, mouth. All that stuff we've been doing. This is not that hard. I just have to forget it's me. And I am not that memorable, so this should be easy.

Right?

Right.

Face is . . . round? Sort of oval? A rectangle. Can a face be a rectangle? Mine can, it seems. But if I do a rectangle, Ms. Rothstein will say I'm doing Frankenstein and flunk me.

So do just oval. I swing my hand around the page, and suddenly, I have an oval. Maybe I can hand this in, say it's minimalist. Or . . . not.

Okay, hair. I glance up at the mirror again. My hair's in a ponytail, just this ridge of dark around my forehead, disappearing behind my ears. My reflection is squinting, saying to me, *That's not so interesting.* I know if I try to draw it, it's going to come out as just this thick dark line around the oval.

Without really thinking about it, I reach back and tug at the elastic band in my hair. It catches, pulls my hair, hurts. I pull harder, and it comes off with a rip of pain and a tangle of torn hair. My hair falls down all around my face, and for a second, I feel smothered. Messy. Sad.

I glare at the mirror, find my eyes behind the hair. There's something wild-womanish about it. Not me at all. But I can look at this without feeling too hideously embarrassed.

Until I hear a knock at the door. I leap up, scrabbling to pull my hair back. Call, "Come in."

My mom comes in. Carefully, like she's not sure what to expect.

"Hi, there." She glances down at the pad on the floor. "Working?"

"Yeah. What's up?"

My mom smiles. "Oh. Phone. For you. I called, but I guess you didn't hear. You were absorbed." She smiles again: *My little artist.* Gag.

"Who is it? Sari?"

"No, a boy. Danny?"

Danny? Danny has never called me before.

My mom asks, "So, are you home?"

"Yeah . . . yeah." I grab the phone. "Danny?"

I hear him say, "Hi." His voice sounds strange. I watch my mom as she slips out of the room, closing the door behind her.

I say, "Sorry."

"That's okay. If you're watching something, I totally get it. . . ."

I say, "No, I was drawing."

"Oh. More *Hollow Planet*?"

"No, dumb school stuff."

"Man, I hate that. When you have to do something you like for school, it kind of ruins it."

"Yeah, it really does." It's weird—when you think something is your own idea then you find out someone else has it too.

For a second, we sit there in agreement. Then Danny says, "Uh, look, uh . . . I was wondering if you'd seen *Bloodsuckers* yet."

"Oh . . ." I feel a twist of disappointment in my stomach, and for a second, I wonder if I can see it first with Sari and then with Danny. But I can't. It's that kind of movie—the person you see it with is the person you're scared with, joke about the cheese factor with. You can do all that once, not twice.

When I give Danny the bad news, he says, "Yeah, I figured you'd already have plans. That's cool."

It's strange, I have never been the person with the power to make another person feel bad. I bet Erica Trager gets off on it, but it feels rotten to me. Like I have the flu.

The next day on the bus to school, I try to figure out if there is any way I can get out of seeing *Bloodsuckers* with Sari. I could say I know she doesn't want to see it, and tell her she can pick the movie. . . .

But that feels creepy. Acting nice, when in reality, you're just being selfish.

Maybe I'll ask Danny if he wants to see something else.

Actually, I think it's good I'm seeing *Bloodsuckers* with Sari. Being a good friend is more important than passion any day.

When I see Sari at the lockers first thing that morning, I feel like it's fate, like the universe is telling me I did the right thing.

I say, "So, question."

Sari is kneeling on the floor, looking through her Tornado bag, but she nods.

"Do we want to do dinner first and see the eight thirty show or rush, see the five twenty, and then have dinner? I'd rather do dinner second and discuss, but dinner after *Bloodsuckers* may not be a good idea. What's *your* opinion? *We'd* like to know," I say, imitating a certain dweeby talk-show host.

That imitation usually makes Sari laugh. But not this time. Instead, she stands up and says, "Actually, bad news. I can't go."

"Oh." This feels much worse than it should, but I manage to keep it out of my voice.

"Yeah, I should have said something before, but today is just totally not a good day. I have way too much work and . . ."

Even Sari knows that claiming she has to do homework is, for her, ridiculous, and she shuts up.

Pulling at her ring, she says, "Sorry, I should've said."

I take one last chance. "We don't have to see *Bloodsuckers*. We could just have dinner—"

Sari shakes her head. "No. It's just that I gotta do

something and . . . you know, maybe another day, okay?"

"Yeah, okay." But now I can't help it. There's anger in my voice, and all Sari can do is sort of smile and walk away.

I wish I could say I am surprised when I see her later that afternoon. I wish I could say I am surprised when I see her walk by David Cole and smile at him and he smiles back, like he used to. I wish I could say that I don't absolutely know whether or not she's going to see him after school today, that that's the something she's "gotta do."

But if I did, I'd be lying.

And right now, I am so, so sick of lies.

For a long time, I just stand there, watching the place where David and Sari were a few moments ago.

I can't breathe. I feel like I'm going to cry, but I can't.

I can't cry because I'm not sad. I'm furious.

She said she would do it—the words are punching into my brain. *She said she would dump him. If he didn't tell Thea, it was over. She said she would never put up with that.*

But she is just a cheap, pathetic liar.

I can't believe that all this time I've been feeling so bad for her, she's probably been seeing David, exactly the same as always. I feel so stupid.

I can feel that my face is all red. So I go the bathroom to wash my face and get it together before class. I don't know if I choose it or if it's by accident, but I get the stall with the Top Ten Sluts list.

After Sari's name, someone has written *Yes!*
And I think, *Good.*

In biology, Ms. Feiffer asks us to identify the muscle in the body that's constantly held in a state of tension.

I want to say, *All of them.*

I can't believe her. I can't believe she just lied to me about it. That she pretended she wasn't seeing David when she was. What kind of freak is she? What kind of sad, pathetic loser?

How can she think we're friends after this?

Maybe she doesn't.

Thank God, thank God, thank God I have no classes with her today. Thank God I don't have to see her again. Because I don't know. I'm where words aren't any good. Unless maybe you scream them.

All I have left today is algebra. After that, I can just go home and figure this out.

I get there early and pick a chair at one of the tables in the back. There's still lots of seats left, so when Erica and her crew come in, they can sit far, far away.

But here's the weird thing: When Erica comes in, she comes in alone. And instead of waiting at an empty table for her crew, she slides in right next to me.

Then she says, "Hi there."

I look around. It can only be me she is speaking to. There is actually no one else at the table.

"I like your pen," she says.

It's my dark green one, the one with the fat nib that's flat on one side, so you can use it for calligraphy. I wonder if Erica would like the pen so much if she knew I have used it to write *Erica Trager sucks* over and over in my notebook.

I decide not to find out. Instead, I say, "Thanks. I like it myself."

I wait for Erica to move. But she doesn't. I think: *Okay, overnight, I must have become popular.* Erica Trager does not willingly sit within five feet of anyone who is not popular. Their Unpopular Germs might get on her, make her fat or break out or something. I mean, it's one thing to talk to someone in the lunchroom. It's absolutely another to sit next to them when you don't have to.

So I must be popular, right?

Then Mr. McGuiness asks us to open our books to page 52. As we do, Erica leans closer—*Watch those Geek Germs, Erica*—and says, "I totally hate math. I am, like, so bad at it."

This is my chance to be cruel. If I want her to go away, I can make it happen by saying, *What are you, like, actually good at, Erica?*

But I don't. I'm weirdly curious as to why Erica is sitting here, risking her coolness rating by quite a lot. (*Sitting next to Jess Horvath? Bzzz. Minus two billion cool points. As punishment, you must ruin your nails and go without hair gel for one week!*)

Instead, I whisper, "I suck at math too."

Erica looks completely amazed. "No way. You are, like, so smart."

Now Erica Trager thinks I'm smart. *Erica, are you on drugs?*

"Can I ask you a question?" Erica asks, not getting that she's already asked me one.

"Shoot." I start drawing short, sharp lines in the margin of my notebook.

"Why are you friends with Sari Aaronsohn?"

At first, I can't believe this is what Erica wants to know. And then I can't believe how I react.

Which is to wonder, *Why* am *I friends with Sari Aaronsohn?*

Answer: *I'm not at all sure.* But I can't tell that to Erica.

Mr. McGuiness asks Matt McCauley to solve a problem. While Matt tries, I mutter, "I like Sari."

"I know, but why? She's so dumb."

Yeah, like you're Einstein's niece, I want to say. But before I can, Erica adds, "Not that I'm, like, any great genius, but she just seems . . . nasty." A little shudder, to make sure I get the point.

"Well, she isn't."

"But isn't she, like, chasing after David Cole?"

So this is the reason for my sudden popularity. For Erica's immunity to my Geek Germs. She wants to know what's going on between Sari and David.

As I think about this, it occurs to me that I should have said something several seconds ago: *I don't know* or *None of your business.*

But for some reason, I didn't.

I feel it swelling up inside me—the yes, the admission, the truth.

Erica whispers, "There's something going on, right? Between Sari and David?"

What is it, this need to tell? This need to see the expression on Erica's face when I say yes? The need to know more than any of them?

Sari thinks this is her little special thing that no one else will ever know or be a part of.

I think: *They only get away with it if no one tells the truth.*

And before I know it, I say to Erica Trager, "That's right."

12

Gaping in astonishment, he staggered backward. His hand outstretched as if to wave off the evil before him, he whispered, "You? It was you?"

—*Hollow Planet: Destiny's Sword*

The second the words come out of my mouth, I think, *Wait . . . Did I really say that out loud?*

Then Erica says, "I *knew* it," and my chance is gone. Even if I wanted to, I couldn't take it back. It's happened. It's all out in the open now.

Erica's about to ask me something else when the teacher asks her if she has something she has to say to the class.

For a split second, I'm terrified she will say yes. *Yes, Mr. McGuiness, I do. David Cole is cheating on Thea Melendez with Sari Aaronsohn! Jess Horvath told me!*

But she says no, and Mr. McGuiness goes back to writing on the board.

The second his back is turned, Erica grabs her pen, scribbles *When?* in her notebook.

I shake my head. Somehow, if I don't say anything more, maybe what I did say will just . . . disappear.

Erica writes, *Please?*

I shake my head again.

Then Mr. McGuiness calls on Erica, and she leaves me alone for the rest of the class.

When class is over, I grab my stuff and run out the door. I'm about to make a break for the stairs when Erica catches up to me and takes hold of my arm.

"I totally understand you can't say anything else. I totally get that. But you should know that Thea is really upset."

I stop. "What do you mean?"

The hallway is filled with kids. Erica pulls me over into the corridor that leads to the emergency exit, so no one can hear. I step behind the fire hose, while Erica leans against the wall opposite. It's like we're in a war, hiding from the bombs or something.

Then, when the halls clear out and everyone's gone, she says, "Thea has asked David, like, a hundred times if he's cheating on her."

"What does he say?"

"The bastard always says no, that she's the only one."

"I can't believe that." I think of David in art class. How he can be really nice. How can he be such a lying creep?

Sounding almost like a normal person, Erica says, "I know. Isn't he the world's biggest jerk?"

I nod.

"I bet he told Sari that Thea has no clue."

"Sari wants him to tell her," I say. This is sticking up for Sari, isn't it? Sari does want Thea to know. And Thea should know.

Erica shakes her head. "He is being such a jerk to both of them."

I can't believe this. Suddenly, the only person in the entire world with whom I completely agree is Erica Trager.

But then I remember . . .

Sari told me, "Tell no one!"

And I have just told Erica Trager.

Who will absolutely tell Thea.

Who will then . . .

Erica glances at her watch. "Oh, my God, you know what? I am insanely late."

Instantly, I know. Erica's not late. She just wants to get away from me as fast as she can and tell Thea all the gory details. I feel sick. For a second, I think of begging her not to tell Thea. But I can't. The whole point of this, from the time when Erica first sat down next to me to now, was Thea finding out.

And now she will. And who knows what happens then.

I give Erica this half smile that she kind of gives me back. And we return to being two people who hate each other's guts.

As Erica walks away, I think: *Did I really do what I think I just did?*

And the only answer that comes back is: *Yes. You did.*

I manage not to see Sari for the rest of the day. I'm terrified that as I leave school, I'll run into her and David.

She will kill me when she finds out. She will *kill me.*

Then I think, *What do you care? Sari LIED to you. She said she wasn't going out with David and she was. She said she would tell Thea and she didn't.*

I try to hold on to the rage for a second, the anger that says this is Sari's fault and not mine. But I can't.

On the bus ride home, I think maybe I can tell Sari I did it for her. Because she wanted Thea to know, and I thought that was the best way for her to find out. Which is sort of true. It was partly what I was thinking. Maybe if I say that, Sari will not stop talking to me for the rest of my life.

At home, every time the phone rings, I jump, thinking it's Sari calling to tell me to die and go to hell.

I don't sleep at all. I cannot stop thinking about what I said to Erica. I can't believe I let those words out of my mouth. Why didn't I just keep my mouth shut? Staple my lips together? I want so, so badly for time travel to be real, to just go back to five seconds before Erica sat down next to me in algebra and do it all over again. This time, *keeping my mouth shut!*

I have to face something: Sari's going to hate me. There's no way she won't find out. And when she does, she'll never speak to me again. Except to say . . . I don't know, I don't even want to think about what she'll say. Whatever it is, I'll have to sit there and take it. Because I deserve it, whatever it is.

It's not even like I can apologize. You can't apologize for something like this. It's not an *Oops, sorry, I take it back* kind of thing.

It's an *I hate you, you ruined the most important thing in my life* kind of thing.

And there's nothing I can say.

Why did I do this? What is wrong with me?

The next day, from the second I walk into school, I can tell: Last night, Erica Trager called everyone she knew and said, *Guess what? David Cole's fooling around with that skank, Sari Aaronsohn. And I know because* Jess Horvath *told me!*

Please, God, I think. *Please, please let her not have said that last part.*

As I walk up the stairs to my locker, I see Kara Davis and Nancy Wein whispering. When they see me, they stare. Stop talking.

I just keep walking.

Everywhere around me, there's a weird buzz in the air, like it's the last day of school. I put my stuff in my locker. Behind me, I hear someone say, "I think she absolutely did the right thing. . . ."

I look up to see who was talking, but whoever it was is gone.

Closing my locker, I look for Sari. But I don't see her.

Maybe she cut school.

Maybe that's why I'm not seeing her.

Or maybe she didn't, and I'm just the last person she wants to see.

In French class, I overhear Lea Figuroa tell Ava

Haverstock, "Erica said she was totally freaked."

"Well, God, wouldn't you be? You could catch something nasty. . . ."

They start laughing. Madame Balmain tells them to *fermez les bouches*, and I don't hear any more.

In gym, as we're lining up to get picked for volleyball, I hear the girl behind me whisper, "She is *such* an idiot to believe that. . . ."

I move closer, try to hear more. But then I get picked and have to run over to the other side of the gym and pretend like whacking a ball is the most important thing in my life.

After gym, I follow the girl into the bathroom. She tells her friend, "He says he was drunk."

"Oh, like that's an excuse."

"Please, I saw her; she was all over him."

I can't figure it out. Are they talking about Thea and David or not? Why would David say he was drunk? Is he claiming he was drunk every time he saw Sari? Who would believe that?

I wonder if David Cole will ever realize that I'm the one who told about him and Sari. I wonder if I'll ever have the chance to tell him how much I wish I hadn't.

At lunch, I sit in the most anonymous corner possible and wait for Sari to show up. But if she is at school, she's lying low. I don't blame her either. Everyone's talking about it. Saying they don't believe it, it's so awful. Or it's so awful and they always knew it would happen. Some people are saying Thea's a snot, other people that David's a jerk. But everyone seems to agree on one thing: Sari is a total skank.

The kids sitting near me are talking about it. Leaning in, all excited, one girl asks the group, "I have to know—what did he *say?*"

Her friend, this snotty, superior chick, says, "He says it was just that one time—"

The others interrupt, all talking at once: "What one time?" "When?" I want to tell them to shut up, that I really need to hear the answer.

"New Year's. At Erica Trager's party."

I stay very still, willing the cafeteria to be silent so I can hear what comes next.

"He said that was it?" The girl who was all excited looks suspicious. "'Cause I definitely heard there was more going on."

Ms. Know-It-All shrugs. "Not according to him. He said Sari probably went off on some ego trip, telling people something was going on."

Her friends snort. "I can believe that."

Later, as we leave the lunchroom, Ms. Excited asks, "How did Thea find out, anyway?"

I stop by the soda machine, try to look like I'm extremely focused on my choice of beverage.

Then I hear someone say, "Who knows?" And for the first time today, I feel like I can breathe.

But that feeling doesn't last long. All around school, people are saying stuff about Sari. Calling her a slut. Calling her dumb. Desperate. Trampy. I want to scream at them: *You don't know anything. You don't know anything about her.*

But I can't. I'm the one who told them everything they know.

Just before my last class, I run down to the lobby, where's there a pay phone. I dig two quarters out of my pocket and dial Sari's number. The phone rings and rings and rings. Either she's not home or . . . or . . .

Where is she?

I hate this. If this is what not being friends with Sari feels like—really not being friends, because she hates me—I can't stand it.

All through my last class, I think: *If I were Sari Aaronsohn, where would I be?*

Answer: *As far away from Jess Horvath as possible.*

Okay, so where does Jess Horvath go to find Sari Aaronsohn?

I don't think she stayed home. It's just not her style. So, if she's at school, I could see her by the lockers at 3:30. But if I don't see her there, then what?

Sari won't go home. I know that. Whenever she's upset, she comes over to my house.

So why hasn't she asked you if she can come over today?

Because she knows. She knows you're the one who opened your big mouth and wrecked everything.

No, she doesn't!

I have to believe that. I have to believe that, somehow, Sari doesn't know.

Where do I go if I'm Sari? My mind flashes through every place she hangs out. Her places are my places, I know them all.

And then suddenly, I know.

The park. The wall by the park.

It's a part of David, and I absolutely know Sari will want to be near something that's close to David.

After school, I get my stuff and head straight for the park. It's one of those weird April days, when nature forgets it's supposed to be spring, and it's blowy and cold and you wish you hadn't put your winter coat away. I stuff my hands in my jacket pockets, hunch my shoulders.

There is a scene in the second *Hollow Planet* book where Rana addresses this underworld crime organization, the Council of Twelve, to try to get them to join the uprising. She walks into their lair, and there's this great description of how they're all watching her from the shadows. She doesn't even know if they'll let her speak or if they'll blast her the minute they get her in plain sight.

Which is basically how I feel right now.

Standing on the corner, waiting for the light to change, I look for Sari on the wall. I can't see her in any of the popular places. For a second, I wonder why I ever thought she would be here in the first place.

Then, as I'm crossing, I look down the street for cars, and I spot her. She's sitting way down at the end, almost where we sat the day we watched David practice and had that stupid fight.

I walk very slowly down the block. Sari's staring off at the empty field, and she doesn't hear me coming. A few steps away, I stop. Call out, "Hey."

She turns her head. For a moment, we just look at each other. Then she says, "Hi," in a voice I don't entirely recognize.

I wait, but she doesn't spit at me. So I get up on the wall next to her, but not too near. Sari looks down at her

shoes as if they are suddenly fascinating. I can't tell—
does she know or not? Hate me or not?

I ask, "Are you okay?"

She shakes her head.

"What happened?"

"You know what happened." I freeze, thinking now
it'll come, the screaming, the fury.

Then Sari says, "It's all over school." She looks back
toward Eldridge like she wishes she could wipe the
place out. "Somebody told that idiot Thea."

"Oh, man." I can't tell, but I don't think my voice
sounds guilty. "What did David do?"

"He never wants to see me again." She looks out at
the field. "He's totally furious with me." She kicks the
wall. "He says I knew the rules and I broke them. He
said if I ever open my big mouth again, I will be seriously, seriously sorry."

I say, "God, I'm sorry." And only I know what I'm
apologizing for.

Sari bites her lip. "I can't take it. I swear."

"Yes, you can."

"I can't. I can't do this. I cannot be without him."

I start to say, *You're so much better without him.* But
before I can get the words out, she turns on me and
hisses, "Stop trying to make me feel okay about this.
You don't know what this is. You don't get it."

"I do get it, Sari."

"No, you don't. You never have. You don't have a
clue." She spits this last word out. "Nobody knows him
like I do."

"You don't know everything about him, Sari."

"Well, you don't know *anything*, believe me."

Very quietly, I say, "That's not true."

"Oh, puh-leeze."

"Oh, really." I look up, look her straight in the eye, so she knows I'm about to tell her something real.

Maybe it's that stupid phrase, the one that reminds me of everything Sari's trying to be, of everything she's not. I want to hurt her. I want to smash the pretty little vision she has of her and David as the center of the universe. I want to scream, *The rest of the world exists! We all exist! You are not the only one who knows things! In fact, you don't know anything.*

I say, "I talk to David Cole, like, every other day, Sari. He's in my art class. He sits next to me all the time." I shrug. "Wow. Big deal."

I like the way Sari looks now, all uncertain and off balance.

"And you know what the big surprise was? He's not that bad a guy. He can actually be sort of cool. When he's not *trying* to be. When he's just a human being."

I know it's coming; I know she will strike back. So I talk faster, hardly thinking about what I'm saying.

"But you know what? I don't think you care about that at all. I think you're just hooked on the idea of going out with Mr. Stud, of getting Thea Melendez's boyfriend, and having everybody say, 'Wow, isn't *she* amazing. Look who *she's* going out with.'"

There's long silence. The longest, I think, that's ever been between us. Then Sari whispers, "I knew it. I totally knew it."

At first, I don't know what she's talking about.

Then I remember.

"When it happened, I thought, 'No way. No way would she do that.' But then I kept thinking, 'Who else? Who else could have told?' You were the only one. The only one I trusted." Her voice is rising. "But I couldn't figure out why. And now I know. . . ."

Sari gets off the wall, stands staring at me. "I know because you're jealous. And you're pathetic. And you're sad. You have no life, and you can't stand it that anyone else has one. But you know what? It doesn't matter anymore. Because as far as I'm concerned . . ."

She steps closer, until she can almost whisper it in my ear.

"As far as I'm concerned, you do not exist."

I wait for a long time. I stare down at the pavement. I try to figure out how many coins I have in my jacket pocket. I try to remember the words to this dumb song my dad used to sing me. And then, when I'm absolutely sure that Sari's gone and I know that she can't hear me . . .

That's when I cry.

13

> The ship glided inexorably through the darkness of space, carrying her farther and farther from the known world. She thought of what lay ahead and saw only a vast emptiness.
>
> —Hollow Planet: Desert of Souls

Here's the thing: Sari doesn't hear me crying and come back and say she's sorry.

I don't call her that night and say how sorry I am.

Monday at school, we don't "accidentally" bump into each other and just sort of start talking.

At no time do I have that moment when I think: *This is stupid. What are we fighting about?*

The fact is, we're not really fighting. Friends fight.

We're not friends anymore.

I'm not sure we ever were.

The next day at school, it's like I'm invisible. I go to

classes, eat my lunch, but nobody talks to me, nobody says, *Hi, Jess.* They're used to seeing me with Sari. Now it's like I've disappeared.

People walk by me, people I'm pretty sure usually say hi to me. Like Zoe Haas, she usually says hi. But today, she just rushes by, like she's late for class.

Or she's just embarrassed to talk to me. The traitorous cow who ratted out her best friend.

I don't see Sari much. We know each other's schedule too well. It's easy for me not to be where she is and vice versa. In English, we sit on opposite sides of the classroom, basically pretend we don't know each other.

It doesn't feel terrible. On the bus ride home, I wonder if somehow, this is my real life. Like my whole friendship with Sari was some kind of dream. When I think about what we used to do, laughing, hanging out in my room, talking about the guy you'd spend your last night on earth with—it seems like scenes from a dumb movie I'd never go to.

Sitting alone on the bus, watching the world fly by as we rumble through the park . . . this feels right. The silence feels right. Nobody watches as I get off at my stop. And that feels right too.

The next week is harder. The next week, I see people. There are cracks in the silence, and I can hear the talk again.

In the bathroom, I hear, "I just totally don't get why *her*? It's not like he could really like her."

"He probably wanted someone he could have power over."

"Right."

"Someone who wouldn't complain or make a problem with Thea."

A snigger. "Well, that didn't quite work out, did it?"

I can feel Sari not looking at me in English. Feel her hating me. I've never had anyone hate me before. It's a very strange feeling—like fingers pressing hard on your throat, wanting you to die.

It gets so bad that one time, I can't go to English at all. I just sit in the third stall of the girls' bathroom until it's all over.

I start avoiding my locker. In the morning, I carry all my stuff around until the 10:00 break between classes. I catch people looking at me and wonder if they're thinking I'm a jerk.

One morning I'm putting my stuff away, I see Danny down the hall. He's talking to someone else, but I can't hear what they're saying. They laugh, and I want more than anything to be with them, laughing about what they're laughing about.

As I lock the door, I think at Danny: *Come over here. Say hi to me.*

When I look up, Danny and the other guy are gone. And I don't know whether he saw me or not. If he still thinks I'm okay or not.

But the worst, the absolute worst, is art class. I am terrified of David Cole now. I sit as far away from him as possible. I tell myself it's because it wouldn't be fair to Sari to be friendly with him. But the truth is, I'm scared to death Sari told him it was me who told and he'll say something awful to me. I hate myself that I care.

But David hasn't said anything to me. In fact, I don't think he even notices me. He's quiet all throughout class, no jokes, no nothing—very un–David Cole like. I don't get it. Thea didn't break up with him. Most people still think he's a god. Some of his jerky friends even think it's cool he cheated on his girlfriend. He's right where he was before—at the center of the galaxy known as Eldridge. So why's he looking so miserable and pissy?

We're working on our self-portraits, and I think he's having a real hard time with his. One time during class, Ms. Rothstein stops by his chair, and he says, "I don't think I can get this."

Ms. Rothstein leans in to help him. I wish I could hear what she's saying, because frankly, I don't think I can get this either.

They say suffering creates great art. But it's not doing a thing for me. Since the whole thing with Sari, I've done a million self-portraits, and every one of them is worse than the last. They range from a squished squirrel to something that closely resembles a rotting grapefruit. Now I'm back to square one. Or I should say, oval one. A big round blank on the page.

When Ms. Rothstein stops to look at my work, I show her my many attempts, the squirrel and the grapefruit. She frowns, but in this nice way, like she's been there and knows what it feels like.

She points to the squashed grapefruit. "I think you were on to something with this."

"Yeah," I say. "Putridness." Maybe that's right. Maybe I am putrid.

"Look here and here." She points to the eyes, draws her finger around the outline.

I shake my head. "I can't see it. I can't see myself, that's the problem."

"Well, that's the hard part." She pats my shoulder. "Don't try to capture everything at once. Focus on one part of yourself. Not your earlobe, but . . . well, why not? If your earlobe is the most you part of you, start with that. Okay?"

I nod. But I want to ask her: *How can I see myself when I've become invisible?*

I look over at David Cole. He's tearing something out of his sketch pad. Slamming his hands together, he crushes it into a ball, hurls it into the corner. Ms. Rothstein pretends not to see him, goes over to help another student instead.

After class, I go and pick up the ball of paper David threw away. I smooth it out, trying to get the creases out as much as possible.

It's not that good, but it's good enough for me to see how ugly it is.

Carefully, I crumple it up again and put it in the trash. It feels like a private thing, and I don't think anyone should be looking at it.

Later, I see David on the corner with some of his friends. A few of the guys are laughing, but David's not. He's standing at the center of the crowd, but it's sort of like he's surrounded. I watch his face, and that's what he looks like: trapped.

Here's what really bothers me: It's not that I told

someone about Sari and David; it's why I told. Because I wanted to feel important. Because I wanted to feel like I was more in the know than Erica Trager, more powerful than David, more fascinating than Sari. More something than every one of them. I wanted to feel like I had something to say. Instead of listening all the time.

I keep trying to tell myself that it was really David Cole who did this to Sari. Or that she did it to herself. But it doesn't work.

When I get home, I go to the kitchen where my mom keeps a calendar by the phone. I count how many days are left in the school year. There are forty-two. Somehow, I have to find a way to survive forty-two more days.

In my room, I get out my notebook and make a list:

Things to Look Forward To
1. Hollow Planet: The Film

But I have to cross that out. The *Hollow Planet* movie doesn't come out until summer.

1. . . .

I tap my pen against the spiral binding of the note-book.

1. Sari talking to me again

I cross that one out too.

1. Doing really, really well on my self-portrait. Learn how to draw real people.

I write that down, stab a big definite dot at the end of the sentence.

That night after dinner, I sit down on my bed with my sketch pad, far away from the mirror, and close my eyes. I think of my face, what I remember first, what I see first. What tells people looking at me that it's me they're looking at?

Then an image comes. I open my eyes, and before I can think about it, I draw a huge circle on the page and begin.

I draw for almost an hour. I only know that when I slow down and glance at the clock. Then it's like I've come out of a trance, and I realize that in front of me, there's some kind of vision of . . . me.

Quickly, I close the pad and put it on the floor. I don't want to see what I've done. If I hate it, I don't think I can stand it.

I decide I really need a soda and head to the kitchen. As I approach the living room, I see the light's on. I know my dad's working in his study, so it can only be my mom. For a second, I hesitate. I really don't want to deal with her right now. On the other hand, I don't feel like I can go back to my room, either.

I could just rush past, pretend I don't see her. But she'd probably stop me. So instead, I stop by the door, like I was looking for her, and say, "Hi, Ma."

She looks up from the book she's reading. "Hi, you." She pats the couch next to her. "Come talk to me."

I go to sit down near her. My mom can be stupid about certain things, but she's smart about knowing when you have something going on that you don't want to tell her about. I don't want to tell her about Sari. It's not something I can tell anyone. So I will have to be very, very careful.

She says, "You've been hiding out in your room a lot lately."

"I have a huge amount of work to do. Art stuff."

"Oh?" She sits up, all interested. "What're you working on these days? I haven't seen anything in a long time."

Yeah, I think, *because everything I do you think is either silly or gross.* "I'm trying to do a self-portrait."

My mother nods, like, *Hey, this is more like it. No more snake men and vermin queens.* "Ambitious."

"Well, it's not my ambition. I have to do it for class."

"How's it going?"

I blow a raspberry, and my mom laughs.

"You'll get it, honey. I know you will."

"I wish *I* knew it."

She pats my hand. "Hey, you're very talented."

I don't think my mom has ever said that to me before. Not like this, as if I were someone she didn't know, someone she'd read about. Staring at my sneakers, I say, "Talented for a kid or for an adult?"

"Well, right now, you're a kid, so it's hard to say. But I'd be very surprised if you weren't talented as an adult, too. You just have to keep growing, taking some risks. Like this picture."

"Well, I hate this risk." I want to kick the table. "I don't know what I look like."

I suspect my mom will think this is idiotic. But instead, she just says, "Hmm."

"I tried looking in the mirror, but it didn't work. I mean, I don't know if I'm pretty or ugly or nothing or—"

"People aren't just pretty or ugly, Jess. Look at the great portraits, is that the first thing you see?"

"So, you're saying I'm ugly."

My mom laughs. "No."

"Well, what do you think I look like?"

"Hon, you're my daughter. You've been beautiful since day one."

"Oh, *great.* I bet that's what the Elephant Man's mom said too."

"I doubt it. Sweetie, I could tell you all sorts of things about the way you look. I could talk about your mouth, which probably feels too big to you now but is going to look so great to you a few years from now. I could say that I wish you wore your hair down more, because you have such pretty hair. I could talk about how I'm so happy you got your dad's eyes and not mine. But that's all a mom talking, and this isn't a mom portrait, it's a self-portrait."

"So that means I have to do all the work."

"I'm afraid so, baby." She smiles, moves close. "So speaking of hair and eyes and stuff . . ."

"Yeah?"

"Who's this Danny? The one who called?"

I look up at my mother and realize she is thrilled. Thrilled that finally, a genuine boy has called her little girl. That her little girl will be dressing up and going on dates and jumping on the phone every time it rings. That her little girl is finally going to be a normal little girl, not the freak that's been living in her house for fourteen years.

I mean, it's been weeks since Danny called, and she's been waiting all this time to ask. I guess now she figures she finally got her chance.

I fight the urge to shriek in her face.

"He's just a guy from school. Heavily into computers and *Hollow Planet*."

My mom nods encouragingly: *More, more. I want details, give me more.* It occurs to me: My mother wants to be my new best friend.

"He's also a serial killer wanted by the police in seven states."

My mother does not appreciate jokes like this, and gives me a look to remind me.

"It's no big thing, Ma."

"Who said it was a big thing?"

But it is a big thing to her, and there's no way she can hide it. I have an edgy, weird feeling all over. My jaw feels like it wants to bite.

In this light voice, I say, "Well, you should be glad it's no big thing. You should be completely thrilled that Danny is just my friend. That I'm not into love or dating or any of that ridiculousness. Because would you like to know what happens to girls who are into love and dating and ridiculousness? They get completely and utterly screwed."

I've run out of breath. My throat is all tight. My mom is staring at me like I've just vomited on her.

"I mean, it's all just a big, dumb show. 'Look who I got, look who I'm with.' Status. People don't even like each other. Then, when they get bored with you or someone cooler comes along, you're . . . nothing."

My eyes are stinging, and I have to look away before I start crying.

I feel my mom reaching out, hear her say, "Baby?"

But I'm out of there long before she can touch me.

In my room, I grab the first thing I can—books— and hurl them against the wall. Good, but there's still too much inside. I take more books, throw them one after the other at the wall. I try to break the wall, destroy the books. I don't care anymore.

I pull the drawers out of my bureau, turn them over. They're heavy and can absorb rage really well. But there's still too much.

I kick the side of my desk until my foot really hurts. Maybe I broke something.

Good.

I kick it again, really hard. I hear my mom walk down the hall toward my room, wondering what's going on.

If she tries to come in here . . .

I stand there, staring at the closed door. I'm breathing really hard, and for a second, I imagine I'm holding the door shut with my breathing.

Don't come in, Mom. Do not come in.

She doesn't.

Finally, when there isn't anything more to throw or kick, I pick my way through the mess to my bed. Everything that doesn't belong, I shove onto the floor.

Then I reach over to my night table and get the third *Hollow Planet* book.

A lot of people ask me why I love science fiction so much. Here's what I'll tell them if they ever ask me again: In science fiction, people are either good or evil. If they harm someone, it's because they want to. If they're good and they want to save people, they have the power to do that. There are no screwups in sci-fi. Nobody who would like to do the right thing but can't quite get it together. Nobody who doesn't mean to hurt someone but does it anyway. There's good and there's evil; you love one and you hate the other. And that's that.

It takes me four hours to read the book all the way through. My mom knocks once; I tell her I'm fine but I need to be alone right now. As she leaves, I hear her say something to my dad, and for a second, I feel lonely. With them on one side and me on the other.

But that's just the way it has to be right now.

When I'm ready to go to sleep, I tiptoe through the wreckage to my computer. I always check my e-mail just before bed. I don't expect anything; it's a just a habit.

But when I open my e-mail, my computer makes the little singing sound, and a message in bold pops up. The subject is "100 Days!" and it's from "Nomi28."

Clicking it, I read:

> only 100 more days until Hollow Planet strikes!
> Hey, where've you been?
> Danny

It takes me a weird second to realize I'm smiling.
Quickly, I type back:

exiled. то hideous and distant place.
can't deal. be back tomorrow.

I think for a second, then type:

are you going to try to go opening day?

I hesitate a moment before clicking SEND. Then I
move the cursor up and press.

14

> At last, the two armies met on the battlefield. There was a terrible silence, followed by the first shriek of war. Followed finally by the even more terrible and lasting silence of loss.
>
> —*Hollow Planet: Destiny's Sword*

My finals schedule is truly ridiculous. Next week, I have to live through the following:

> TUESDAY: Biology exam
> WEDNESDAY: History paper due
> THURSDAY: English paper due
> FRIDAY: French exam. Final art
> project due

One thing I can never stand about school is that no matter what happens to you in your real life, you're still expected to get good grades. Even if your entire year has been one big soap opera, no one cares. Not your teachers, not the principal, your parents, no one. You could lose all your limbs and half your nose, and they'd still be, like, *You got a* B- *in history?*

Which is why I'm in the library trying to cram. And I'm not alone. Look around, and everywhere you see heads down, notebooks open, pens scribbling away. You definitely smell panic in the air.

Eric Reed is lurking around the stacks; he says he's got something that'll help you pull three all-nighters in a row, and people keep drifting back there to talk to him. At the table next to me, some girls are whispering about the senior party, comparing rumors about where it's going to be and figuring out how to crash. Their words keep getting tangled up in the *plus-que-parfait.* I turn around, about to tell them to shut up . . .

And that's when I see Sari.

I haven't seen her—seen her and really *looked* at her—for a long time. And at first, I don't recognize her. She's wearing her hair in a braid, which makes her face look seriously fierce. I can tell she's not eating, because she's gotten really skinny. As she stands in the doorway, she manages to look for one particular person and let the rest of us know we can all drop dead at the same time.

I know she's not looking for me, so I glance around the library to see who it is she is looking for. She might be here to study with someone. But something about the look on her face tells me that she's not.

Then all of a sudden, she strides to the back of the

library and disappears behind the stacks. The girls nearby start whispering madly. I hear: ". . . David . . . Thea . . . He said it was only once . . . She's a total liar . . . Skank . . ."

But even they shut up when Sari reappears a few minutes later.

With Eric Reed.

Eric Reed? What's Sari doing with Eric Reed?

Last year, she said he was a druggy jerk.

So why is she leaving the library with him?

And why is his arm around her?

If I find out Sari's doing drugs, I'll kill her. I'll find her, make her talk to me, and tell her what a complete idiot she's being.

After school I bump into Danny on the corner. I'm so lost inside my brain thinking about Sari and how I can find out what's going on with her, I don't even see him until he waves a hand in front of my face.

"Hey." He smiles. "What's up?"

"Oh, hey, Danny." Then, because I'm embarrassed I didn't see him, I ask him if he wants to walk through the park.

"What were you so deep in thought about?" he says as we pass by the soccer field, where some guys are kicking a ball around.

At first, I think, *No, don't ask him. Danny's not going to know anything about Sari.* Then I think, *Why not?*

"Do you know why Sari would be hanging out with Eric Reed?"

Danny looks surprised. "No. I thought she was . . ." He's all embarrassed. "You know, with David Cole."

"That's dead."

He thinks, then shakes his head. "How do you know she's hanging with Eric?"

"I saw her. In the library. These stupid chicks were going on and on about the senior party and—"

Then I stop. Danny stops too, says, "What?"

"Eric is going to the party, right? Even though he's not a senior?"

"Yeah. He always gets invited. He sells to all those guys."

"That's why." Danny looks at me like, *You're making no sense.* "Why she's suddenly all hot on Eric. She wants him to take her. To the party."

Danny nods. "Oh. 'Cause of—"

"'Cause of *David.* God, I can't believe her. How can she want to do that? Those people hate her, they're all friends with Thea. She's, like, totally lost her mind."

Danny shrugs. "Maybe she really wants to see him."

"She just wants to see him at the Big Event. She's always been psycho about the senior party; it's, like, her dream to go."

"I've heard it can be kind of cool."

I blow a raspberry. "Oh, please. 'Oh, we'll never see each other again. Oh, it is so sad. Our wonderful little clique will never be the same. Now we must go out into the real world, where we will become roadkill because we have no brains.'"

Danny laughs. "Oh, come on."

I walk to the side of the path and pretend to barf. As I stand up, I see Danny's looking uncomfortable. He kicks a stone across the path, follows it as it skitters off into the grass.

He says, "Well, then, I guess I shouldn't ask this. . . ."

"Ask what?"

He shuffles his feet, then looks down like he's telling them to quit it. "You think the whole thing is completely lame."

"What whole thing?"

"The senior party."

"What about it?"

"I was going to ask if you wanted to go."

At first, I don't know what to say. "We can't. We don't know where it is."

"I do." Danny grins. "Steve Howett lost all his physics notes on his laptop. I got them back for him. But as payment, he had to tell me the secret lo-ca-tion." He says it like in some crazy spy movie. "So, I thought maybe you'd want to go. But I guess not."

"No, I—" Then I stop, because I'm not sure what I was about to say.

"No, it's okay." Danny starts walking.

I follow, saying, "No, I just think . . . I don't know, maybe we could go."

There, I've said it. Sort of.

Danny looks over. "Really? Even given the lameness quotient?"

"Yeah, kind of even especially given the lameness quotient. Like, maybe it's so lame it has to be done."

Even as I say this, I think: *This is a total cop-out.*

But I'm going with Danny. I can hardly be accused of trying to be cool.

Actually, me and Danny crashing the hallowed senior party, invading their sacred turf with our freakish selves, spreading geekdom wherever we go—it's pretty funny when you think about it.

Danny breaks out into a smile. "Well, great. Excellent."

That night at dinner, it occurs to me that I will have to ask my parents if I can go.

I watch them as they eat, trying to determine the optimum time and approach—that is, the one that offers the least opportunity for my mom to drive me bats.

She will be psycho with happiness. I can just hear her: *You're going to the senior party? Who asked you? That boy, Danny? I can't believe it!*

Then I hear my mom ask, "How's the portrait going?"

"Uh . . ." I pretend to chew while I think. "It's, um, going."

"Can we get a special members' preview?" My mom smiles, and my dad nods.

"It's not actually ready for viewing yet," I say. "But definitely, when it's ready to show."

My self-portrait is definitely not ready to show. But not because it's not done or not good. The picture I did the night I flipped out has turned out to be quite interesting. But I don't want to show it to anyone until I understand it better, because it really wasn't what I expected.

My dad asks how the studying is going. I lie and tell him it's going really well.

Later, as we're clearing the table, I say, "Uh, guys?"

Both my parents look at me. Staring down at the plates in my hands, I say, "Some people are going to the senior party. Is it okay if I go with them?"

There's a pause. Then my dad asks, "It depends on the identity of 'some people.' Sari?"

I shake my head, put the dishes in the sink. "Danny Oriel." I glance at my dad. "He's a perfectly decent human being, I promise."

I steel myself for my mom's explosion of happiness. The shrieking . . . the hugs . . .

My mom says, "Sure. Just not too late, okay?" Then she starts taking dishes out of the drying rack.

After a second, I help her.

Sometimes my mom is not completely terrible.

Over the weekend, I study like mad for my biology final. I read about reproduction, how sperm fertilizes egg, how chromosomes divide, become zygote, become fetus. So that's love.

I read about arteries, how they carry oxygenated blood from the lungs to the heart to the rest of the body. How once the heart stops, the oxygen to the brain stops, and the brain waves cease. So that's death.

And then it's all over, and I'm done.

Done with freshman year.

I didn't even fail. Not a single class.

At least, I don't think I did.

The very last thing I do on Friday is hand in my art project. I wait until the end of the day to go to the studio. Ms. Rothstein is washing out old coffee cans we use to clean the brushes. I wonder what she does with them at the end of the year. Throw them out? Save them?

I put my portrait between two pieces of cardboard to protect it on the way to school. I'm not really sure how to present it to her, so in the end, I just hand it to her, say, "I did it."

For a second, she holds it, then looks at me like she's asking permission. I say, "Sure, go ahead."

I'm about to add, *Just don't tell me if it sucks.* But I don't. Because I know it doesn't, and it would sound stupid to say it. Like I was forcing her to compliment me. That's something I get now. That I should leave people alone that way, let them think what they think.

She works her fingernail between the pieces of cardboard, breaks the pieces of tape on either end. Then she takes off the top layer. For a long time, she just looks. I see her eyes moving, but I can't tell what she's thinking from her expression.

Here's what the portrait looks like: What I first drew, when I was trying to think of what really looked like me, was a huge mouth. Which I thought said everything about what I had done: opened up my mouth and spilled everything all over the floor in a big, disgusting mess. I thought it would be like a baby crying, some horrendous brat demanding to get fed. I didn't expect to like it when I looked at it again, but I thought it would be the truth, that it would help in some way.

But when I got up the nerve to look at it again a few days later, I didn't see any of that. There was this huge open mouth, but it was more like a scream, almost a storm. Around it I drew my hair from that time in front of the mirror when I took it out of the rubber band, when it was all tangled and impossible and I hated it. And some of the pain of pulling it and getting stuck ended up in the picture, and my eyes are shut, and you know I don't want to look at myself—but what you really know is that I want someone to look at me.

I've looked at it a few times after finishing it, and I always see that. And that's why I don't think it sucks.

Ms. Rothstein is grinning at me. She puts the picture down on the table.

She says, "You really did do it." Then, "How does it feel?"

I don't quite know the right words. So instead, I grin back at her, and she bursts out laughing.

Ms. Rothstein says she'd really like to display some of the portraits in the school lobby; would I mind if mine was up there?

"Ugh. Everyone would see it."

She smiles. "Well, you're going to have to get used to that. Sooner or later."

I see Sari only once on the last day of school, and it's from far away. I'm heading to the library to return some books when I spot her at the end of the hall. She's about to go into the stairwell, probably to go home. Her Tornado bag is slipping off her shoulder, and she stops to adjust it.

And all of a sudden, I remember last year, when it was so hot and sticky and gross, and we went to any dumb movie we could find . . . and then the first day of school, walking around these halls like it was a whole new world and hiding out in the back of the gym at assembly because only suck-ups sit up front. . . .

And I really, really miss her.

I've been to just one party before. And Erica Trager's party was all about getting together and being this little group. But the senior party is the last time some people will ever see one another. It's all about good-byes, and that's why these parties get crazy.

For a second, I think of calling Danny, telling him I don't want to go. But then I think of Sari on her own in the hallway, and I have the strongest feeling that it's very important for me to be there tonight.

One thing about cool parties: They're always in dumb places it takes forever to get to. This year, the senior party is in this old factory space all the way downtown. On the subway, I joke to Danny, "Maybe it doesn't exist. Maybe it's like Dahj—this eternally shifting world that disappears just when you think you're there."

He laughs. I can't believe how calm he is. Sari would be all tense and weird.

I know she's going to be there tonight. I just know it.

I have to admit I feel somewhat tense and weird myself. What are people going to say when they see us there? What are they going to think about me being with Danny? I seriously hope no one makes any obnoxious comments.

I have to be positive about this. Who knows? Maybe they'll throw us out.

The street is dark and deserted except for the glow from the open front door of the factory, which lets light spill onto the street. Some people are hanging out on the steps, sitting on cars and drinking. No one says a thing as we pass and start walking up the stairs.

The party's on the top floor, and with every floor, I can hear the music getting louder and louder. Even two floors below, I can hear people screaming and laughing.

I shout up to Danny, "Whoo-hoo—par-tay!"

He grins over his shoulder, and I feel better. At the door, I steel myself for the person who will tell us to get lost. But we pass right into the crowd, like we're just anybody.

"You want something to drink?" Danny shouts.

I nod. "A soda."

I want to go with Danny, but I know I'm supposed to wait for him to bring the soda to me. I fold my arms in front of me and fight off anyone who might be staring at me by staring right back.

Cautiously, I examine the space. It's one of those places where there's one big room for dancing, and then a lot of little rooms that don't make any sense. A lot of people are just hanging out in the hallway, waiting to see who comes in next. Everybody's all mixed up out here; laughing, screaming, drinking. I look around for Sari or David or even Thea, but I don't see any of them.

The Prada Mafia is here, waiting by the door to see all the senior gods show up. They're clumped together, with Erica at the center, like they're sticking to her. Erica sees me and waves; a little wave, so her drones don't catch on. Immediately, she cranes her neck to see beyond me, and I know she's looking for Sari. Unconsciously, I turn and look for her too.

Then I feel Danny nudge my arm, two cups in his hands.

"Hey." I take one of the sodas.

"Sorry, it's kind of nuts." He raises his cup. "Well, here's to . . . something."

"Here's to doing lame things."

"Yeah, absolutely." He grins, and we clink cups. I'm about to say we should go check out the other rooms when there's this big burst of screaming and hugging at the door. I stand on tiptoe to see who's here. Then the crowd breaks up a little, and I see . . .

Couple of the Year: David and Thea.

It's strange—when David and Thea are together, they look like they're straight out of a TV show. If that's a great thing to look like, I don't know. But they make most other people look . . . average. He's got his arm around her shoulder, and he's kissing her, like, every five seconds. She's leaning against him, holding the hand that's on her shoulder.

The Prada Mafia is going berserk, looking at David and Thea and whispering away.

"Oh, my God, they're here."

". . . and, you know, *she* might be here."

"Can you believe it . . . ?"

". . . so bizarre . . ."

All of a sudden, I feel Erica Trager standing next to me.

"Hey." All friendly, like we're best friends. Then she lowers her voice. "Did you come with Sari?"

I shake my head. "Nope."

"Well, do you know if she's coming?"

I shake my head again.

Erica presses. "But she probably is coming, right? I mean with . . . *David* here."

"I really don't know, Erica." I almost scream it.

Some song starts up in the next room, and suddenly, everyone's whooping and running to dance. That's when I see my escape and grabbing Danny's hand, I pull him into the dance room. It's pitch dark and vibrating with music and hundreds of people pounding away on the dance floor. For an instant, I feel totally lost; what did I come here for?

Danny jumps onto the dance floor and starts leaping around like he totally knows this song, totally knows how to move to it. I feel more frozen than ever, unable to move until he gestures, *Come on.* I glance around; all these people staring. But there's Danny, and I can't say no. He got us in here. So I take a few steps forward, and before I know it, I'm on the dance floor.

I have to move. Everyone else is, and if I don't, I'll be decapitated by a flailing arm or knocked over with a full-body blow. Basically, at first, I'm just jumping to avoid people. That, and to save my life. Then I watch Danny and try to jump with him. The song launches into the chorus, and everyone roars along. Danny too. I don't know the words, so I just laugh.

Then I glance around. Nobody is watching. Nobody cares.

For a second, it occurs to me: *I am at a party. And I am having fun.*

Very strange.

Another song starts, some speedy, boppy thing, and people start dancing like crazy. It's like the whole room hit fast-forward, and I'm swinging and twisting like a madwoman just to keep up. I'm aware of the crowd swelling like a wave, as everyone goes, "Whooaaa. . . ." I'm pulled away from Danny as the crowd separates into two halves, then crashes back together. Everyone dances backward again, then charges forward, laughing hysterically. It's part of the dance. I see Danny fading back, reaching his arms out, and I do too. I run back with everyone else, but this time, I can't find him.

I nudge my way to the side, try to spot Danny in the crowd. I'm just wondering if he went to look for me somewhere when someone taps me on the arm. I turn and there's David Cole.

He points a finger. "I saw what you did."

For a split second, I know absolutely that he's talking about Erica Trager. But before I can say I'm sorry, he says, "In the lobby. Your Rothstein picture. How come you didn't tell me you were so good?"

It takes another second for me to understand what he's talking about.

I say, "Um . . . I didn't actually know that I was."

"Not going to forgive you for that." Then he grins. "Come on, dance with me."

I look for Danny, but I can't find him. Meanwhile, David is lifting up my hands, gently kicking at my feet, so I have to move them.

"Yeah, that's it." He swings my arms, like we're doing some corny old fifties thing. I can't help it, I laugh.

Whatever the joke is, we both get it, because he laughs and then we start making the same moves.

We're both imitating the same old dance, so we know how it goes and know when to goof on it. And all of a sudden, I get it. Why everybody likes David Cole. Why Sari likes him. How he can make you feel like it's just you and him. And all the rest of it—school, parents, the whole game—is sad and silly and boring, and the least you can do is laugh at it.

Other people start dancing around us: David's friends from the soccer team, Charlie, Sasha, and Tobin. Then some girl, Leslie somebody and Debbie. I feel David's hand break from mine, but then I feel him nudge me with his hip, like I'm still here. But a few seconds later, he's dancing with Leslie, pretends fighting with Tobin. I'm still moving, but I feel out of sync. A little silly.

Finally, the song ends and everybody cheers. I smile *Thanks* at David. But he's already moving off with his little crowd and doesn't see me. Behind his back, I wave good-bye.

Then I go look for Danny. I find him coming back into the dance room. Seeing me, he starts, says, "Hey."

"Hey yourself. Where'd you go?"

"I don't know." He grins. "I kind of got carried off. Then I realized you weren't around, so I came looking for you."

Something about him saying that feels good. I say, "Well . . . cool."

"So . . ." He gestures toward the dance floor. "You feel like dancing some more?"

They've put on a sappy slow song. Couples are sleep-walking around the floor, all wrapped up in each other.

Shy, I shake my head, hoping Danny doesn't mind. Across the room, I see David lead Thea out onto the floor, holding her by the hand. There's a burst of cheering and applause as they start to dance.

And then all of a sudden, I see her. Sari. Dancing on her own around all these couples. Most people would look very strange doing that, but not Sari. She's a great dancer. I don't know what it is, she just knows how to move. She goes off in her own little world and just connects with the music like she doesn't care who's watching her.

Like she has no idea that David and Thea are just a few feet away.

David's got his head down, nestled in Thea's neck. I don't think he's seen Sari. But Thea has. You can tell from the way she's staring straight ahead, keeping her back to Sari, totally pretending she's not here.

Other people aren't pretending. All around, you can hear this hum of voices—some excited, some low and pissed off.

"Oh, my God . . ."

"I cannot believe this."

"What is she doing?"

Right near Sari, there's a group of seniors hanging out by the window. Like, there's Charlie and Tobin, and Andy Schwartz and Leslie, who's Andy's girlfriend. They're staring hard at Sari. Sari ignores them.

Leslie walks over, like she's going to get something to drink. She bumps into Sari—supposedly by accident.

Leslie says, "Oh, sorry." But her voice is nasty.

Sari stops dancing for a second. Then she closes her eyes, starts moving again.

She's moving closer to David and Thea. Other couples are moving off the dance floor. No one knows what to do.

I want to grab Sari by the arm and drag her out. I want to yell at David, *See? See what happens when you play with people? Look up and see for once!* I look at Thea, furious and trying not to cry, and I want the whole stupid thing never to have happened.

Sari's not pretending she doesn't see them anymore. Now that it's just the three of them, she's opened her eyes, and she's looking straight at David, like, *You can't just make me go away because you don't want to deal with me anymore.*

Then all of a sudden, Thea just stops. She quits dancing completely, says, "Come on, David."

"No, it's fine." He takes her arm, starts moving his feet around. But Thea doesn't move.

Slowly, Sari stops dancing too. And waits.

Thea says, "I mean it, David."

Everyone's watching. I don't think anyone can breathe. Thea gives David a long hard look, then she walks off the floor over to Leslie, who hugs her and helps her disappear into the crowd.

For a long terrible moment, David and Sari just stand there. Sari's hands are in fists at her sides. Her jaw is rigid, and her eyes are shining. She's waiting for David to look at her, waiting for him to admit she's there.

But he doesn't. Instead, he kind of shrugs. For a second, he smiles down at the floor, and I have this weird memory of him in art class when he knew he just couldn't do it and he didn't know whether to laugh about it, get pissed off, or what.

Then he turns around and walks off after Thea.

At the sight of Sari all alone, I gulp in air, start toward her. But I'm not fast enough. In the silence, someone—I swear it's Erica Trager—lets out a shriek of laughter. The sound of it hurts my ears, maybe even my eyes, because suddenly, I can't see Sari clearly. I can see her walking quickly, but not running, never running, and then all of a sudden, we're next to each other. I put my arm around her and we head right for the door. Once we're out of the party and away from the laughter, she puts her head down like she never wants to see anything ever again.

We are standing on the street. At the corner, Danny is finding us a cab. Sari's eyes are huge. Tears are all down her face. She looks so fragile, like she's gone somewhere deep inside herself. Or else just flown away into the night sky when no one was looking.

She says, "I don't want to go home."

"You're coming to my house."

She nods.

In the cab, she closes her eyes. Her head rocks against the seat, and her mouth's a little open. It's like she's asleep, but I know she's not.

Danny whispers, "Will she be okay?"

I nod.

We sit for a while, watching the city speed by, the lights streaking past like dashes of water. The river looks flat, secretive, like someone's just slipped beneath the surface and drowned. I want to be home more than anything.

"Hey," I say.

Danny looks at me.

"Thanks a lot."

He smiles, looks out the window to hide it. "Maybe next time," he says, "we'll go to a movie."

Here's what I'm praying as I unlock the door to my house: that everyone will be fast asleep.

I can deal with Sari. I can deal with my parents. But I cannot deal with both at the same time.

It's 2:00 in the morning. I feel like I haven't slept for a year.

The key keeps slipping. I can't remember how to turn it.

One more try . . .

Finally, I make it. The key turns, the lock clicks, the door opens. Without a sound, we creep down the hall-way to my room. Sari goes into the bathroom. I follow, shutting the door and turning on the light.

Immediately, almost like she couldn't take another step, she sits on the side of the bathtub. I wet a towel and touch it to her forehead. I try to wipe her cheeks and her forehead. Then she hiccups.

I can't help it. I laugh.

Sari takes the towel and hiccups again. Then she laughs too. Sort of.

"You okay?"

"No." Sari hiccups. "Not at all."

She tries to smile, but the smile slips. "I can't believe that happened."

I'm about to tell her that it doesn't matter. That she'll get over it. And who cares about David Cole, anyway?

And I know all that's true. But instead, I take the towel back, wet with hot water, and give it to her to warm her face. Because I think right now, that's all she wants.

I get out my futon chair, pull my sleeping bag out of the closet. In my drawers, I find a T-shirt for Sari to wear. It's the same one she always wore when she slept over, the one with a big sloppy dog on the front. Once it's on, she looks down and smiles.

It's funny—I'm completely tired, but once I get into bed, I feel wide awake again. I stare up at the ceiling, imagine that I've just been tossed onto shore by a huge wave and I'm looking up at a night sky full of stars.

I hear Sari say, "There's only this one minor, tiny problem."

"What?"

"I don't think I can ever go back to school again."

"Don't be dumb."

I hear her head slide against the pillow as she looks over. "God, could you?"

"None of them will be there next year," I say, meaning the seniors.

"Other people will be."

"Yeah, I will be."

"That's true."

We're quiet for a while. Then I say, "Hey, we could do the Book. Ask it what next year will be like."

Sari laughs. "No more Book. I don't want to know what the future is; it's too scary."

"Okay."

But I know that sometime in the summer, she'll stop being scared. I know that sometime, she'll start wondering what next year will be like. And I know that she'll want to do the Book. So I'll keep it under my bed, where it's always been.

Some things you lose, and it's better.

But some things you keep.

15

Victories came where they were not expected. Defeats too. But in the end, their forces had emerged intact. Ragged, battered, but still loyal.

—*Hollow Planet: Thorvald's Hammer*

At 3:30 on the morning of July 12, I'm standing on the corner, waiting for Danny. I've never been out this late before, never seen the city so still and deserted. While I wait, I pass the time by imagining I'm waiting in the woods for allies to come.

Then I hear someone say, "Hail."

I say, "Hail" back.

Danny grins. "So you think we have a shot at getting in?"

"Let's go see."

For its opening day, *Hollow Planet* is showing at one theater only. When we were trying to decide when to get on line, Danny and I figured that either people would be waiting on line for weeks before, which even we weren't prepared to do, or that we might have a shot if we went early, early in the morning.

At first, Danny said we should meet at the theater. But I told him I couldn't stand being disappointed immediately if there were a million people there. Which is why we met a few blocks away instead.

As we walk, my stomach's all tight, and I tell myself not to be ridiculous. *It's just a movie. What does it matter when you get in? When you see it?* Everyone gets in eventually. But some things are just really big. Some things you want to be a part of. And as sad, pathetic, and geeky as it is, the opening day of *Hollow Planet* is one of those things. For me, anyway.

I think: *We should have left earlier. Midnight. I bet a million people came out at midnight.*

Just before we turn the corner on to the last block, I take a deep breath.

Danny says, "Ready?"

I nod. "Ready."

We turn the corner.

There is a line outside the theater.

But it's only about a hundred people. Which means we're going to get in. We rush to the end of the line and drop onto the pavement with a big sigh. Some people ahead of us smile, and we wave back.

I settle in, rest my head against the building. I am going to see *Hollow Planet* on opening day.

Then I hear Danny say, "Hey, what if after all this . . . ?"

"Yeah?"

"What if it sucks?"

I think: *Then we will be among the very first in the entire world to know that.*

At 10:00, we file into the theater behind other cheering, whooping fans and watch *Hollow Planet: The Film.*

It doesn't suck.

In fact Danny and I are going to go again this weekend.

It's funny—I still can't believe I'm going to be a sophomore.

Last year feels so over. Like it all happened long ago, when I was a little kid.

The Saturday night before school starts, I go over to Sari's for videos. We order an obnoxious amount of Chinese food, sit back on huge pillows, and watch movies until our eyeballs hurt.

During the second movie, Sari points to the screen and says, "That guy kind of looks like David."

It's the first time she's mentioned David all summer.

I say, "Yeah, maybe. A little bit."

Sari picks a dumpling out of the carton, eats it with her fingers. I slurp a cold noodle.

Then I ask, "Do you ever miss him?"

Sari frowns. "I used to. A lot. I don't know. It's dorky, but he was really exciting to be around." She looks at me. "That's sad, right?"

I shrug. "It's true."

"Yeah?"

"Yeah." I don't look directly at Sari when I say this, but I can feel her smile.

"Still," she says, "I was pretty pathetic."

"Oh, definitely."

"A complete loser."

"Lost soul."

"And, of course, you were too."

"Well, of course."

We laugh. Then we watch the rest of the movie.

While we're rewinding the tape, Sari asks, "Hey, whatever happened to that picture?"

"What picture?"

Sari puts her hands on her hips. "The one you were drawing of me."

"You weren't supposed to know about that."

"Oh, yeah, like you were so subtle." Sari hunches over, imitates me scribbling and peeking with huge eyes.

"I never got it good enough."

"So, try again."

"Now?"

"Sure." She flings herself back on the pillow. "I wish to be immortalized."

"I don't have my stuff."

"I've got stuff." She jumps up and hunts around for some paper and pencils.

Handing them to me, she says, "Please?"

I shrug. "Well, you did say 'please.'"

Sari flops on the floor and strikes a pose. I say, "Not like that. Be normal."

Sari giggles. "I am so not normal. Oh, hey, hey . . . I have an idea. Do both of us."

"Both?"

"Yeah. You know, together. The artist and her extremely strange friend."

I think for a moment. "Okay. But I have to do you first."

"Cool. And you have to show me when you're done."

"Cool."

"No hiding it away in a drawer."

"No hiding it away. Now, shut up and let me think."

I bend over and concentrate on the page. Then I look up, touch the pencil to the paper.

I am drawing a picture of Sari Aaronsohn.

Who is my best friend.

Here's a sneak peek at
Mariah Fredericks's next book.

Don't miss *Heavy Breathing*!

1

All it is, is a little pressure.

And just like that, everything changes.

You think about all the channels, all the wiring. The signal from your brain running through your nervous system to the tip of your finger. From the mouse through the cable, then ... out there, miles and miles of electricity, snapping and crackling down the line, and then it all comes screaming right back at you.

And there it is, your answer.

Which might explain why I've been sitting here for three minutes, unable to do something as simple as bend my finger.

Just a little pressure ...

Nope, can't do it.

I've got the cursor in place. It's right over the dice symbol, ready to give me the number.

I'm just not ready to ask for it.

I think about numbers. One through six. How much difference is there between one and six? Between two and five? Three and four? Almost none.

Out of the corner of my eye I see a new message.

Scared?

I resist the temptation to type the symbol for the finger sign.

Because I am. **Scared?** But he doesn't have to know that.

There has to be a connection between the noun *die* and the verb *die*. It can't be a coincidence that this little cube of chance has the same name as the ultimate bad roll.

Three is not death, I remind myself. Four is not death. Neither is five or six.

Only one and two.

I've earned a four or a five, I think. I've been playing really well.

And I've been attacked. And by someone on my team. That should earn me something, right?

But you can't earn anything in a game of chance. Luck isn't earned. It just is.

It just is.

Time to throw myself upon the mercy of the universe.

I think: Click. But my finger doesn't move.

Another message: **If you kick a dog and it doesn't move—is it dead?**

I type back: **If you kick a dog, it might jump up and bite your ass.**

I think: Things you can make happen with just a finger.

Shoot someone . . . drop the bomb . . . piss someone off. . . .

Pick your nose.

I smile.

Okay, do it now, do it now with a smile, do it with a finger up in his face, do it.

No one or two.

No one or two.

Threefourfivesix. Threefourfivesix.

I fix my eyes right on the screen. No looking away. Press.

After all that, it's easy. Just press and it's done.

Can't take it back now.

Snap, snap, screaming through the wires, the question, the answer, the request, the reward or the punishment.

What do we have for her, what do we have?

We have . . .

Four.

And I am still alive.

My mom knocks on the door, tells me it's time for dinner. I tell her, "In a minute."

She opens the door. "Judith. *Now.*"

■□■□

Now I am here.

"Here" is the kitchen. "Here" is the plate on the table. Salt and pepper shakers. The mail stacked up on the counter. My mom eating.

I am here now, me again.

But the Game's still in my head. Buzzing and crackling, like in the Frankenstein movies, where they shoot the monster up with electricity.

There was a 33 percent chance I could have rolled a one or a two. If I had rolled a one or two, I would have been stuck with a very low level of strength.

Irgan, the guy who attacked me, rolled a three. But he has an extremely high level of aggression. Aggression can mean you don't need as much strength.

I can't believe he attacked.

Can't believe I actually survived. . . .

My mom says, "You sit too close to the screen."

My mom—the other person at the table obsessed with the Game.

"It's really not good for your eyes," she says.

I nod over my plate.

"You think I'm nagging, but I'm not."

I smile. "No, I know."

But she is. Nagging. The problem is not the screen. Or my eyes.

My mom just hates the Game.

She sighs dramatically. "I remember when people used to play games with other people."

"I do play with other people," I remind her.

"I mean people you can see. People who are there."

"They are there," I say patiently. "They just happen to be in other places while they're there."

Like Timbuktu. Or Anchorage. Or Third Avenue.

Now, if I had rolled a three . . .

My mom's voice. "Do you know anything about these people? Who they are?"

"What does it matter?"

"It does matter," she says. "It matters because there are sick people out there."

Mom's biggest fear. Perverts on the Internet.

It's a joke. The new bogeyman.

I should make a joke, actually. Something about monsters under the bed.

But for some reason my throat's tight—whatever I say, it'll come out wrong. It's the images in my mother's head. Drooling old men reaching out to put their hands on you. Their gross, sticky fingers. *Come here, little girl.*

Joke. Think of a joke.

I grin. "Well, then it's definitely a good thing that there's a lot of distance between me and them."

"And you'll keep it that way?" She's all intense. "Someone asks to meet you, you say no?"

"I say no."

For a few minutes we eat. My mom tries to decide if she's satisfied, while I try to be as small as possible, give her no target. I know we're both thinking, Why do we have to fight about this? Except my mom's also thinking,

If only she'd quit, and I'm thinking, If only *she'd* quit.

My mom is not the worst. She tries. Only sometimes too hard.

Then from the outside hallway we hear the rumble of the elevator, someone getting off on our floor. Our kitchen's right by the front door, so you can hear everyone coming and going.

Well, you can hear the Heitmans. They're the only other family that lives on our hall.

My mom pretends to be eating. But I can tell she's listening. Trying to figure out: Is it Mrs. Heitman? Mr. Heitman? Or Jonathan?

It's almost nine o'clock. It could be Mrs. Heitman coming home from work.

It can't be Mr. Heitman coming home from work. Mr. Heitman doesn't have a job.

Could be Jonathan. Coming home from wherever.

The door to the Heitmans' apartment opens. Closes.

My mom waits a second, then says in a low voice, "I saw her the other day."

"Who? Mrs. Heitman?"

My mom nods. "She looked completely exhausted."

I shake my head and Mom shakes hers, too. We may not agree on the Game, but we do agree about Mrs. Heitman. We feel bad for her. And we like her. Even though we don't know her that well.

We should, when you think about it. Know her better. The Heitmans have lived next door as long as we've been here—practically forever.

But the Heitmans aren't really the kind of people you know. They're the kind of people you stay away from. Not Mrs. H., but Mr. Heitman sort of. And Jonathan *definitely*.

My mom reaches across the table and squeezes my hand. Like, *Maybe my kid spends too much time on the computer, but she's not a psycho like Jonathan Heitman.*

Then she gives me a big smile. "Hey, when's Leia coming around? I miss that girl."

I take a drink of soda. I wish there were a way, when you don't ever want to think about somebody again, that you could erase the memory of their existence from other people's minds. Because as long as they're in someone's head, they exist. Which means you end up talking about them.

Which means you have to remember they exist.

"I mean, now that the school year's started, and you guys are back at Connolly, I'm assuming you'll be as inseparable as ever."

Lie or tell the truth?

I can't decide, so I end up not saying anything.

"How was her summer?" My mom's still on it.

I concentrate on my plate. "I don't really know."

"You don't know?"

"No."

My mom frowns, then asks, "What? You guys have a fight?"

"No, we just . . ." I shrug. "I don't know."

She waits for a second, then says, "Well, whatever it is, I can't imagine you won't work it out."

I nod. Because I don't know what else to say.

"Maybe you should give her a call."

"Yeah, I *did*." That comes out wrong, and I start forking up carrots.

It's a weird thing: When you get loud, everyone else gets quiet. I can feel my mom dying to ask, "So? What happened?"

But instead she changes the subject. And I let her.

Because she's right. She really doesn't want to know.

Later, as I wash the dishes, I think about aggression. When someone attacks and they're stronger than you . . .

Way more aggressive than you . . .

How do you fight back? How do you win?

What can you use to defend yourself?

Intelligence, for one thing. Weaponry, obviously.

Luck.

I'm not sure if I have luck or not.

In fact, I'm fairly sure I don't.

You can always start over, I tell myself. It is only a game.

Only it's not.

2

My great-uncle Albert was called Crazy Uncle Albert because he was a genius. At least, people thought he was a genius because he was good at math, and no one could figure out how his mind worked. Actually, it didn't work a lot of the time. There were basic life things he couldn't do, like drive a car or talk to people.

But his mind worked really well when it came to numbers. So well that during World War II the government sent him to Los Alamos to work on the bomb. After the war he taught at a college. But then he just kind of lost whatever normal mind he had and became a hermit somewhere until he died.

We have one picture of him. He's your classic dork.

High-water pants, glasses, weird crew-cut hair. He's standing in some field with his shoulders back, like someone told him, "Pose for the camera." I guess he meant to stick out his chest, but the first thing you see is his stomach.

He looks like a nice person, though. He's got this big smile, like he's thrilled someone would want to take his picture.

My mom says I'm like him. She says that's where I get my "math mind."

I don't *look* like him, and I hate to be mean, but I'm a little glad about that. Not that I would say this to Mom about her uncle, but . . . no harm in thinking it.

My dad said that to me a few years ago: "There's no harm in thinking." We were talking about Crazy Uncle Albert and whether it was right to use your brain to build weapons.

He said, "You can't expect people not to think. Not to know things just because they *could* be bad."

I said, "Yeah, but then they built it and a hundred thousand people died."

My dad laughed and said there were a lot of steps between the thinking and doing.

Which I know, duh. All I was saying is that when you think of doing something, you don't always know the consequences. For a while people *thought* about building the bomb, but nothing happened. In the end it was a lot of different people doing a lot of different things, most of which had nothing to do with the bomb, that did make it happen.

I think about that sometimes. Who was the person

who had the first thought, the one that started it all?

And after they had the thought, what was the first thing they did?

I know my uncle never thought, Hey, all this great science—one day I'll use it to kill a whole bunch of people. You just look at his picture; he's not that kind of guy.

And yet, I guess in a way he sort of is.

On the next page of the scrapbook there's a picture of my dad. He's a little kid, standing in a yard in front of a big house. That's just one picture of him; obviously we have more. Him and my mom, him and me. But nothing for the last five years. Not since he moved to Seattle, where he got a job at a university.

I used to think of my dad and think of a smell. His sweaters had this rough, woolly smell, and when you hugged him, you just breathed it in.

Now I think of a voice, "Hey, kiddo." Which is usually the first thing he says when he calls. He calls me every week.

Sometimes when I talk to him on the phone, I try to picture him in his house talking to me. If he's sitting down or walking around. Doodling.

And sometimes I think maybe he isn't in his house. Maybe he's in his car, or another state. Or another part of the world. Maybe this is just a tape.

That's when I say something bizarre like, "I thought I saw a lizard on the crosstown bus the other day," something no computer could think of a response to.

Just to make sure.

■ □ ■ □

Right now all I'm thinking of doing is raising my hand.

Action: Raise hand in math class.

Consequence: Get answer wrong. Look like complete moron.

I think I'll keep my hand down.

It's easy to look like a moron in this class. It's full of extremely smart people. Because I'm here, I'm supposed to be one of them, but I can't help feeling someone made a big mistake. And that any second now Mr. Jarman, the teacher, is going to figure that out.

On the very first day he said, "I expect you all to participate. That means speaking up, taking part. Anybody who thinks this class is about tests and homework is wrong. Math is dynamic. Math is about risk. You can't be afraid to be *wrong*—even in front of your classmates."

That's really when I should have raised my hand. *Uh, Mr. Jarman? Sorry. I don't do those things.*

Because all that sounds great, right? But the thing is, at Connolly everyone is hypercompetitive. About everything. Money. Looks. But mostly intelligence. If you're at Connolly, you're supposed to be smart. Like . . . the best. Whatever that means. Kids who are in the top ten of the class want to be in the top three. Kids in the top three want to be number one. I don't know what number one wants to be. Probably a professor at MIT.

So if you get something wrong in front of your

classmates, it's not like they're going to go, "Oh, that's really interesting, let's talk about that." They're going to go, "Ha, ha, you suck."

Be invisible—that's my solution. Do my thing, but basically, if no one knows you exist, no one's going to try and come after you. I'm not a star, one of those kids on Mathletes or a statewide prize winner—and I want to keep it that way.

Now Jarman's prowling around the classroom, waiting for an answer.

I really should raise my hand. Get it over with. It's the second week of school, and practically everyone's had their hand up at least once but me.

I'm pretty sure I know the answer.

So, just raise your stupid hand.

Maybe I'm paralyzed. Because my brain is telling my hand to move, but my hand's not listening.

Perhaps it knows my brain doesn't mean it.

Raise your hand!

I lift my fingers off the table. But just as I'm thinking, Rise, Sir Wrist, Peter Nardo's hand shoots up, and Jarman shouts, "Yes, Peter!"

Great. Peter Nardo was the only other person in class who hadn't said anything yet.

Now I'm the only one left.

I get through the rest of class okay. But as I get up to leave I can feel Mr. Jarman watching me.

You're next.

■□■□

One day I'm going to invent a game called *Lunchroom*.

Lunchroom: Where no one survives.

You could have evil counter ladies, toxic food, spaghetti sauce spills that make you stick to the floor. The line that NEVER ENDS! The vending machine that EATS YOUR MONEY! The foul stench that KNOCKS YOU UNCONSCIOUS!

Your challenge is to make it through the crowd and find a safe place. Various things can kill you, from putrid veggie burgers to the explosion of laughter that occurs right after you drop your lunch tray. And every person you see, you have to figure out friend or foe, threat level, potential for alliance, and so on.

Like right now, coming at me is Ray Girardi. Won't hurt, won't help. He's a neutral.

But on my left is a table I call the Isle des Snobs. They can freeze you if you get too close. Avoid at all costs. Next to them is the Mathlete crowd. They look like potential allies, but they're all in Jarman's class and have an interest in wiping you out as a threat. Assess risk. Decide not worth it.

Allies are almost never worth the risk.

I spot an empty table in the far corner. It's right by the vending machine, which is why no one wants it. But it's perfect for me.

One problem: I have to pass by Leia to get there.

The ex-friend who GIVES YOU THE LOOK OF DEATH!

And Leia is not alone. Leia has allies.

Namely, her new best friends, Kelsey and Jessica.

It's funny, until the end of last year Leia never even mentioned K&J. They were completely off her radar. But this year you'd think they'd all been buds since first grade. They do everything together. Lunch. After school. They even tried to get the same classes.

They laugh the same way too, at the same time. Then they laugh about how they laugh.

And to get to my safe place, the gross, sticky table by the vending machine, I have to walk past all three of them.

Okay. The thing to do is pretend complete ignorance of their existence. Like my mom says about people I play the Game with: "You don't see them, so how can they possibly exist?"

Also, do not breathe while passing by them. Ex-friends can emit poisonous gases.

Basically, be invisible.

They do see me—I know because they stop giggling for two whole seconds—but they pretend not to. No snickers, no nasty comments. This time, anyway.

Maybe Leia thinks I have a high threat potential.

Yeah, right. She just refuses to acknowledge that you exist.

Well, same here.

Finally I reach the table, where I pull out my Game notebook. In it I keep a record of my moves and the moves of certain other players. It helps me strategize. Also, to ignore people.

As I look over my notes from yesterday's game I keep thinking about how my mom's always worried some creep from the Game will hunt me down and kill me.

And now someone *is* trying to kill me.

I don't get it. What does Irgan the Head Case want with me?

There's a burst of laughter, mean laughter; some poor soul just got zapped. Even I look up to see who it is, and that's when I see Katie Mitchell standing at the outer edge of the tables, her tray tilted, a huge splash of soda on the floor next to her.

Katie. Of course.

In *Lunchroom: The Game* definitely one of the weakest levels of player would be a Katie. The fat, rich girl who tries too hard to get people to like her, so of course nobody does. Katie's a total airhead. Airheads don't do well at Connolly.

Everybody says about Katie that her parents got her into Connolly because they gave a lot of money to the school. Which is a horrible thing to say about anybody, but she's such a dip you kind of believe it.

Right now she's faced with that most dire of *Lunchroom* scenarios: nowhere to sit.

Last year she could have sat with Kelsey and Jessica. They were her "friends" last year, even though K&J made it clear that Katie should feel honored that they let her hang with them. I guess she agreed, because she never seemed to mind how they put her down.

Then at the end of last year Leia started hanging around

with Kelsey and Jessica. Guess who was odd girl out?

As Katie wanders around looking for somewhere, anywhere, to sit, she glances over at Leia and K&J, but they totally ignore her.

I'm about to go back to my notebook, when Katie looks over, sees me watching her, and breaks into this huge grin.

Oh no, I think. No, no, no . . .

Too late. Katie's headed this way.

"Hey, mind if I sit down?" She doesn't wait to hear yes, just sits. "Being Psycho Student Woman, I see." She nods at my notebook. "God, I haven't even, like, *started*. I think my brain is still on vacation. What brain I actually have."

This is how Katie talks. Nonstop. Like if she stops for air, you'll tell her to get lost.

I have no choice. I put the notebook back in my bag. So weak I can't even defend myself against Katie Mitchell.

"So, what's up?" Katie smiles and bites her lip at the same time. "You have a cool summer?"

"Yeah, pretty cool."

"I went to Maui."

"Whoa." Which, I think, is the right thing to say.

"Yeah, kind of sucks if you're not Bikini Goddess, but hey. Decent shopping."

She nods. So I nod. And think, Katie, what are you doing here?

But I know what she's doing here. I don't even have to look at Leia and her pals snickering to know.

Katie glances back at where they're mopping up her

soda spill. "Could you believe I did that? God, I am, like, Klutz Woman today."

I say, "I've done it a hundred times." I haven't, but why be a jerk?

"I probably ruined my shoes." She looks down, all upset.

Okay, that's it. Maui is one thing. Shopping and Maui—maybe okay. But I am not going to listen to shopping, Maui, and shoes just so Katie has someone to sit with at lunch. Just so she can pretend she has a new "best friend."

I start getting up. "You know, I have to go. I've got this huge test coming up."

Katie nods. Like she totally expected to get blown off. "Sure. Hey, maybe I'll see you around."

I nod back. Escape, escape . . .

Of course, I don't have a test. No one does the second week of school.

But I do have a psycho killer on my butt, and if I don't figure out how to get rid of him, I may be dead in four hours.

Three thirty. One hour to Game time.

From Connolly to my house it's twenty-three blocks. Twenty down and three across.

Last year I always walked the same way.

And I still go the same way this year.

Which means walking past 158 West Seventy-first Street.

Some numbers are ill omened. They have their own particular energy. You can actually feel it sometimes when you come across them. It's heavy, oppressive. Like the feeling in the air right before a storm.

With 158 West Seventy-first Street it's something about the combination of numbers. They feel out of sync. Nothing quite fits with anything else and nothing wants to. There's all kinds of cracks and fissures in the surface. It's not a solid gateway. A lot can get through.

Sometimes, in order to make my way past it, I tell myself it's just a door. It's green, it's got gold numbers on it—158. That's all it is, just a door.

I remind myself that it's daytime. Broad daylight. Everyone can see everything.

Ill-omened things can work *for* you, I tell myself. It's not a bad thing to come in contact with a destructive force, absorb some of its power.

Still, I hate walking on Seventy-first Street.

Leia Taplow lives on Seventy-first Street.

But that's not why.

It doesn't matter why.

Today I walk right by it without looking. But I know when it's coming, and right before, I feel myself speed up, walk just a little faster.

I hate myself for that.

Tomorrow I'll do it again, exactly the same way. Only I won't run.

I glance at my watch. Start walking faster.

Almost Game time.

> > mariah ♥ fredericks

...as born and raised in New York City. She went to a school quite like Eldridge ...ternative, though they called it the Calhoun Learning Center. The school had ...o walls, but remained standing nonetheless. Later she attended Vassar, which ...id have walls.

She has never lived anywhere else, but she has visited Lenin's Tomb in Moscow, and other famous places with dead people in them. She has had a lot of jobs, and most of them involved books. She has reviewed books, shelved books, and sold books. "Writing books," she says, "is definitely the best job I've had so far."

Mariah still lives in New York City. Only now she has a husband and a basset hound, as well as a lot of books. Don't miss her next novel, *Heavy Breathing*, coming soon from Simon & Schuster.